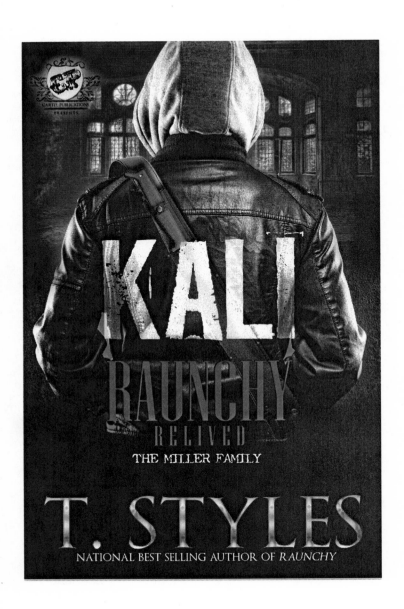

CARTEL PUBLICATIONS
PRESENTS

KALI

RAUNCHY RELIVED

THE MILLER FAMILY

T. STYLES

NATIONAL BEST SELLING AUTHOR OF *RAUNCHY*

ARE YOU ON OUR EMAIL LIST?

SIGN UP ON OUR WEBSITE

www.thecartelpublications.com

OR TEXT THE WORD: CARTELBOOKS

TO 22828

FOR PRIZES, CONTESTS, ETC.

CHECK OUT OTHER TITLES BY THE CARTEL PUBLICATIONS

4   By T. Styles

WWW.THECARTELPUBLICATIONS.COM

KALI:

RAUNCHY RELIVED

(THE MILLER FAMILY)

BY

T. STYLES

Library of Congress Control Number: 2015952838

ISBN 10: 0996209905

ISBN 13: 978-0996209908

Cover Design: Davida Baldwin www.oddballdsgn.com
www.thecartelpublications.com
First Edition
Printed in the United States of America

What's Up Fam,

I hope you all had a great summer and are ready for fall and the upcoming holidays. I can't believe its football season again and almost time for Halloween. Time really flies so please make the best of it. Don't waste precious time on negativity or dreams lost. Get out there and make it happen. You never know what tomorrow will bring.

Now, on to the book in hand, "Kali: Raunchy Relived". I could not wait for this book to drop! I loved how the beautiful and talented T dot Styles took us on a journey into Crazy Kali's background and how he became the psycho he is. She did an outstanding job on this one and really took her time. I'm certain you will agree and love it just as much as I did!

With that being said, keeping in line with tradition, we want to give respect to a vet or a trailblazer paving the way. In this novel, we would like to recognize:

Suzy Favor Hamilton

Suzy Favor Hamilton is a former Olympic runner as well as a

By T. Styles

former high-class prostitute turned author. Her novel, "Fast Girl: A Life Spent Running from Madness" is a New York Times bestseller that details how she went from an Olympian to tricking in Las Vegas all while being a wife and mother. It is an extremely open story on Suzy's trials and tribulations and the illness that caused her to lead two different lives. Check it out!

Aight, get to it. I'll catch you in the next novel.

Be Easy!

Charisse "C. Wash" Washington
Vice President
The Cartel Publications
www.thecartelpublications.com
www.facebook.com/publishercwash
Instagram: publishercwash
www.twitter.com/cartelbooks
www.facebook.com/cartelpublications
Follow us on Instagram: Cartelpublications
#CartelPublications
#UrbanFiction
#PrayForCeCe
#PrayForSeven

#KaliRaunchyRelived

By T. Styles

"The sins of the father are to be laid upon the children."

- William Shakespeare

By T. Styles

PROLOGUE

PRESENT DAY

Hard rain, orchestrated by violent thunderstorms pounded on the navy blue van as it veered down the dark winding road. It was the type of weather that made one believe that God was through with mankind, leaving every wretched soul to fend for himself.

Inside of the rocking vehicle, eyes blindfolded, arms tied tightly behind their backs, were three strangers. Although different circumstances brought them together, they sat arm in arm, simmering in the smell of feces and fear. Each wondering how fate would have its way with their lives.

When the van made a sudden stop, Kali Miller's body knocked against the man on his right, and when it started again he drifted into the man on his left. Earlier each was stripped of their shirts and shoes by the abductors before they made the trip to their unmarked graves, within the soft dirt of a Virginian woodland. The back of the van, separated from the driver by a metal wall, made it easier for them to speak if they desired, yet no one bothered to say a word.

Until now.

"I wish I knew," Barrie Cody finally said to himself, unable to take the silence, even if it meant hearing his own voice. "I just wish I knew why I'm here." Limited ventilation caused puddles of sweat to soil the white bandana covering his eyes. "I wish someone would talk to me." Anxiety was causing him to loose composure, resulting in heavy breaths laced with uncomfortable anticipation.

Not even two hours earlier, Barrie, a black Irishman, was snatched out of his bed where he lay asleep with his sick wife. All night he nursed her, trying to exterminate the high temperature, which had weakened her body's defenses, bringing her closer to death. As with the others, they snatched his car so that there would not be cause for alarm, at least for 24 hours.

Barrie wondered would he ever see his sickly wife again.

Did the kidnappers murder her or leave her untouched?

"You...you...know what we did," Timo Rupert whispered in his direction. The stutter in his speech softened the passion he felt for each word. "You...you were there with me, forcing me, even though I didn't want to go." Having been the one who released his bowels five minutes earlier in his jeans, he was now filled with hate for his brother-in-law, who in his opinion had been nothing but trouble since marrying into the family a few years earlier. "Now I'm going to die in this...this van and it's all your fault."

"You know, I'm sick of you blaming me for shit!" Barrie roared, over Kali's body. "You wanted in so I gave you your wish. You don't actually think them bitches you fucked would've dealt with you without paper?" he laughed. "Do you?"

Kali was so silent as they ranted that they almost forgot he was sitting between them. Although they all suffered bruises and lacerations, Kali, with his rebellious spirit endured the most abuse. A three-inch gash ran across his forehead and the corner of his lip was busted, the blood held in place by a hardened clot.

Upon hearing Barrie's words, Timo calmed down although he was on the verge of a breakdown. The reason he was involved in the stash house heist, which he believed was the cause for the abduction, was because of his ability to case a scene and assess the risks no matter how protected the property.

From trap houses to city banks, nobody had an eye better than Timo. If there was a caper he could supply the team with foreseeable problems before moving forward, allowing each man in his camp to plan properly. The trouble was he was also a first generation bitch who couldn't be counted on to stay unflustered if things got thick.

"Ya'll talk too much," Kali finally said, unable to bite his tongue. "And niggas who talk too much say more than need be told."

Barrie and Timo sat back against the van's wall; an immediate respect for the soft spoken stranger filled the air.

"I didn't think you knew how to talk," Barrie said sarcastically. "Haven't said two words this entire trip."

"Yeah...what...what you in for?" Timo asked.

Kali laughed softly as he considered the query. A better question would have been what hadn't he done. From kidnapping to murder, a man of his tenure had done it all. "Too many things." His words came out within a deep exhalation, memories of the wicked life he led traced through his mind.

"Just say you don't want to answer, nigga." Barrie was annoyed that the stranger didn't offer more. "It ain't like we not gonna die anyway."

"You may die...but I won't," Kali said smoothly.

"This nigga...nigga...funny. Case you haven't realized it they got you in the back of this bitch right along with us. You...you not going nowhere if they don't want you too."

Kali shook his head. "All my life people have been trying to write me off, even my parents." He considered the irony. "And you know what...I'm still here."

PART ONE

By T. Styles

C.

BERNICE "

Before long I was ha~
no one. Mama alw~
when she not ~
songs la~
to

All eyes were on
surprised because
wearing a white silk ⸱
expected every dick in ⸱⸱ be stiff and
pointed my way.

Standing in the corner of Nellie's house, at her 18th birthday party, I allowed the *Isley Brothers'* voices to move through my soul. As I listened to the words of their hit song *'It's Your Thing'* I waited for the right man to come my way, and if he wanted he could whisper the lyrics in my ear.

I scanned the room and every man worth anything was snatched up, although each would glance at me every so often. Figuring it was time to steal a man I wiggled my hips, softly, from side to side, like blades on a car's windshield wipers. The banging of my gold bracelets clanking together sounded like soft bells as my body vibrated.

KALI: Raunchy Relived   19

ing such a good time I needed

ys said a woman's most attractive

ooking for a man. I guess that's why two

er, after my body moistened, causing the dress

ling to my light skin, Leroy Payne strolled up. Wearing a pinstripe blue suit, he removed a gold cigarette case from his pocket, flipped it open and said, "Smoke?"

Leroy was a pimp, and a cool cat with lots of dough to splash on a chick like me who looked even prettier in pretty things. I felt myself getting overly excited with just the possibility of sitting in his black Lincoln Continental parked out front.

Wanting to appear older than my 17 years I said, "Sho nuff, Leroy." I slid a square from the case, placed it between my plush pink lips and said, "Got a light?"

He winked, removed a gold lighter from his pocket and sparked my tip. I could see him eying the dark circles of my breasts; as the silk rubbed against my skin and caused my nipples to harden.

"You one foxy mama," he said licking his lips.

I could smell his cologne and felt tingly inside. "Thanks," I winked and took a pull of the cigarette.

By T. Styles

Suddenly my chest was filled with a flood of smoke. It was like it entered each crevice of my lungs, making it impossible to breathe. Afraid I was about to die my eyes widened and the cigarette toppled out of my hand before Leroy stomped on it like a roach. I thought I was about to cough up my guts when his massive hand came slamming down on my back repeatedly, like I was a baby.

My knees went slamming to the floor as my body dropped on all fours. "How — *cough* — could — *cough* — anybody smoke — *cough cough* — that shit?" I was losing all of the sexiness I mustered up earlier.

"Maybe little girls shouldn't be smoking," he said as he tapped my back one last time with an attitude.

Standing up halfway I leaned on the wall. "Well, I ain't little." I straightened myself out and tucked my right titty back into my dress that managed to pop out. "I'll be 18 next month."

"Well 18 ain't here is it? And Leroy don't fuck no kids." His eyes rolled over my body again. Maybe he was trying to make up his mind for sure. "Besides, if I did give you the dick you wouldn't know what to do with yourself."

He walked away and I stuck out my tongue at him.

I stood in the corner, arms crossed over my chest, lips pouting more than usual. I'm tired of men telling me I'm not old enough for this or for that. If something adventurous didn't happen in my life and soon, I had visions of killing myself.

I was just about to leave when *'I Heard It Through The Grapevine'* came on the record player. Suddenly my body had wings again. Snaking my hands through my thick curly Afro, I softly swayed my hips from left to right as the song continued to move my body. When I opened my eyes briefly I saw Leroy staring again and when I glanced down at his crotch I noticed his dick was stiff.

Maybe I'm not so little after all.

Closing my eyes again I continued to dance until suddenly I was yanked downward, my lips pressed against the hardwood floor. The record scratched and the music stopped as someone continued to pound on me. It wasn't until the lights got turned up, that I caught the flash of my mother's silver wig.

Now I knew what was happening.

She was taking the dress off of my body, a dress I borrowed out of her closet that she was too wide to wear.

"Look at ya," she said with disdain. "You ain't even lady enough to wear no underclothes." She slapped me again and I covered my face with my arms. Air rushed over my vagina because it was out in the open.

"Mama, don't do this!"

"Don't tell me what to do! You so selfish, Berny, and I'm tired of you. Don't care about nobody but yourself. Here it is I needed help and you out here parading yourself like a whore! You keep this up and you gonna turn into one. Just wait!"

"Mama!"

"Don't bother coming home tonight. I'm done looking at ya."

I glanced her way, just long enough to see the blood stained dress she had clutched in her palm walk out the door.

"Muffy, turn the album back on," Nellie said to her cousin. The music filled up the room and the lights were dimmed. "And everybody finish dancing. The party not over yet." She laughed nervously.

KALI: Raunchy Relived   23

Nellie quickly moved toward me and helped me up by snaking her hands under my pits. When I was on my feet she tried to cover my body with hers by standing in front of me but it didn't stop me from catching Leroy's disapproving glare. I guess more than anything I really was a kid to him now.

Once we got to her mother's room she slammed the door. "Sit on the bed, Berny." She pointed to it as if I didn't see the thing. It was almost as big as the floor.

I flopped down, my bare ass pressed against a baby blue comforter. I felt guilty about ruining her party but at the same time it wasn't my fault my mama popped up, was it?

I could feel her anger and for some reason moved my eyes everywhere but on her face.

Gazing at the dresser I saw a police badge belonging to her father and on her mother's side lots of small glass jars filled with perfume. Taking a deep breath I said, "Sorry about this, Nellie."

Although she said, "It's fine," the way she opened and slammed the drawers as she searched for something for me to wear, told me she was still pissed. Nellie was a big girl so I couldn't fit a thing of hers.

I was still getting my thoughts together when she tossed a white t-shirt in my face, followed by some tiny jean shorts. "On second thought why shouldn't I be mad at you?" She turned around and crossed her arms, tucking her hands under her pits. "This was a perfect night, Berny! And here you go fucking my groove up again. Why would you come to my party in her shit anyway? It's like you love making her mad."

"You know that ain't true!"

"How many times has your mother ruined one of my parties trying to find you?"

Too many for me to count.

"It was supposed to be my birthday!" She continued.

It still was.

"Now all anybody will remember is you sitting on my floor naked! You nothing but trouble and you gotta get your life together before God gives you something you can't handle."

Maybe her words were true or maybe they weren't. Either way I stood up walked toward her and tried to hug her but she backed away like I had the Pox. "I don't have time for that nice shit. Put some fucking clothes on."

I don't know what came over me. But suddenly I slapped her in the face with my entire palm. I was still trying to figure out why I did that when she raised her leg and kneed me so hard in my pussy I thought my period was about to come down. "Oh my God!" I yelled as I doubled over and fell on the floor.

My third time for the night.

When I was down she kicked me in the back of the head and walked toward the door. "You got five minutes to get out my house! And don't let me catch you around here again, I just might kill you."

I didn't leave.

Instead I spent the night sleeping in Nellie's backyard like a dog and now I was sitting at a bus stop with a sheet wrapped around me. Like I just left a toga party. She took her mother's shorts and shirt back and wanted me to walk away naked. I refused knowing she wasn't supposed to be having a party with her parents out of town anyway.

By T. Styles

Nellie going to give me the sheet but only after a neighbor threatened to call the police and scream orgy if I wasn't covered immediately. I didn't want to be there all night but who could I call to pick me up? My mother told me not to come home. My brother's phone was disconnected, so it meant her backyard would have to do until daylight.

When the bus finally arrived I held my purse against my breasts, stood up and eased on. Grabbing some pennies I dropped them into the meter and walked toward the back. Everybody, including the driver, looked my way as I tried to find an available seat.

When I made it to the back I was relieved and blinked a few times when I saw a man who was so sexy he gave me chills. He had a smooth baldhead. A five o'clock shadow. Thick lashes. Chocolate skin and wide eyes that seemed to sparkle. He was pretty and handsome at the same time and I was about to introduce myself, until I remembered I was dressed in a sheet.

It wouldn't have mattered anyway. He seemed unaware of my presence and was more interested in the Hershey colored woman with the thick legs sitting across from him.

Still, for some reason, I couldn't turn away. The only time I blinked was when my eyeballs dried out and I stared some more. I was still in his face until he did it.

Something I hadn't expected or was prepared for.

He snaked his fingers inside his grey slacks, and started beating his dick. My eyes widened more and my jaw dropped because I couldn't believe what I was seeing. Was he actually doing this in public?

At first I thought it was just me and that I was seeing things, because when I looked around no one seemed to notice. Not even the woman he was using as his muse.

As he went to work, still eyeing the lady, he bit down on his bottom lip and jerked harder. It was so obvious now I thought he was going to rip his penis off.

I was disgusted and fascinated.

I guess he was making too much noise because the woman finally focused on him and she didn't seem pleased. "Wait, what the...what the fuck are you doing?"

Caught, he slipped his hand from his pants, pulled up his zipper and turned away as if he didn't know what she was talking about. But I could tell by her attitude that she wasn't going to let the matter rest.

"Don't turn your head now, creep!" She stood up and slammed her yellow patent leather purse over his forehead. It cut his skin because he was bleeding on top of his head. Glancing to the front she said, "Jerry, come back here, you not gonna believe this shit!" She looked at The Jerker. "My brother gonna fuck you up! Just wait!"

Suddenly a large man with arms the size of my thighs stomped toward the back of the bus. His yellow t-shirt seemed too small for his chest and I thought his muscular body would rip the fabric to shreds.

"This jive turkey was whacking off!" She told Muscle Man.

"He was what..." Without another word Muscle Man snatched The Jerker out of the seat. Holding him from behind, his arm was nestled in the pit of The Jerker's neck, his bicep partially covering his nostrils.

And then we waited. Waited for the driver to reach the next stop and once he did Muscle Man yanked The Jerker off the bus with Hershey and me following closely behind.

Why was I there?

I knew it was dumb but I couldn't mind my business.

I was wrapped in a sheet and had problems of my own!

It was weird. Nothing about this man was somebody I wanted to get involved with, yet there I was, watching and waiting for The Jerker's fate. I stood not too far from the fight, like I was the ghost of Christmas past showing The Jerker his life.

"Kick his fuckin' ass!" Hershey yelled. "Do it good too, this mothafucka disrespected me!" Although she lent her suggestion it didn't look like he would stop anyway. I watched Muscle Man pound his face relentlessly, The Jerker's neck clicking back and forth. At the most I thought he would tire and stop his beat down but then she said, "Kill that nigger."

My eyes widened as my mind ticked. This was about to go too far. Yes he was gross and disgusting, but did he deserve to die? Suddenly I remembered I'd stolen a few things last night from Nellie's house. I did it to be petty but I might be able to save his life.

By T. Styles

I rifled through my purse just as I heard a gun cock. Where did the Muscle Man pull the weapon from so quickly?

When I found what I was looking for I flashed it and yelled, "Freeze!"

Hershey and Muscle Man looked shocked, I guess they didn't know I was there. I raised Nellie's father's badge in my hand high like I saw on the movies. When I glanced at it I saw it was upside down and repositioned it right side up. "Unless you want to go to jail don't shoot." My voice cracked but I figured they got the message. "I'm a cop!"

When my sheet fell around my waist, exposing my breasts I started to pick it up. But everything about this situation was dumb so I said fuck it and just let it hang.

CHAPTER TWO
BERNICE

After helping The Jerker, I caught the bus home and of course my mother wouldn't let me inside. She told me since I was wearing a sheet I should sleep in the streets where I belonged. Who does that to their own child? It's so fucking stupid! Instead of begging, which I've done in the past, I decided to go to my brother Grand's house even though I couldn't reach him.

On the way there, riding the bus, I thought about how I helped The Jerker whose real name is Rufus. He smiled after I flashed my badge, causing Muscle Man and Hershey to run down the block. But he didn't show much emotion. I helped him up and the only thing he said was, "Thanks hear."

Not sure why but something about him I liked although he didn't show interest. Instead he stood up, looked at me once and stumbled away. It's just as well, someone that horny is bound to be trouble.

When I got off the bus and made it to my brother's street I could hear loud music coming from his house.

Mind you it's early in the morning. Grand has a thing about being surrounded by younger women and since he moved out of our parents' house, I can't remember one time when he was alone. He sold heroin out of an ice cream truck, but would spend the money on liquor and women so he hardly had anything left.

When I made it to his house I kicked a few Coke bottles and other trash out of my path in his yard as I shuffled my way to the front door. I took a deep breath, knocked hard and wasn't surprised when a light skin girl with a really high Afro opened the door...topless.

She rubbed her eyes so hard her mascara smeared. "Grand said the party over. Come back tomorrow."

She closed the door halfway when I pushed it open and bum-rushed my way into the house. "Bitch, I'm coming to see my brother." The moment I walked inside I stopped short and looked around. There were so many sleeping bodies lying on the floor it looked like the holocaust. Shaking my head I stepped over them and walked toward the back. "Grand! Grand!"

Slowly the bodies began to move and moan and Red was still behind me. She turned the music off.

"How I know you his sister? You can't be just walking up in here." She placed her hand on my shoulder.

I shoved her so hard she tumbled backwards, her body on top of the others, her crotch hung over their faces.

"Keep your hands off me." I continued as I made my way to his bedroom.

Once I opened the door I smelled what could only be described as crabs from yesterday. There were five bitches on his bed and nestled in the middle was my 27-year-old brother. Slowly he woke up, raised his head, before scratching his bushy mane. "Hey, sis." He tried to sit up but his head fell backwards like it was too heavy for his shoulders. "What you doing here?"

"Mama put me out and your phone turned off."

He sighed, raised his head and shook it from left to right. "Bernice, you gotta do better. You gotta get your life together."

I looked around his room at the foul smelling women, and recalled my trip inside where I was greeted with sleeping naked bodies. He had zero room to talk. "You're right, but I need your help."

"Tell me something I don't already know."

"Stop playing, Grand!" I stomped my foot. "You gotta let me stay a few days."

He sighed. "Fuck! Why can't you do right by ma? Why you keep putting yourself in a twist and expecting me to get you out? My spot ain't no rest haven for little girls, Bernice."

There he go with that "little girl" shit again. I rolled my eyes and said, "Please, Grand. You let me stay and you won't even know I'm here. I promise."

His body dropped back to the bed, and one of the women, who still looked sleep, placed her forearm on his neck. "You got three days."

A sense of relief took over. "Thank you..."

"Don't thank me, just remember the rules. Leave my weed alone. Leave my money alone. And don't irritate any of my bitches, especially my favorite."

"Who's that?"

I felt someone tap me on the shoulder and when I turned around the redbone who opened the door slapped me in the face.

It had been two days and staying with my brother was hell. He had a party every night and there was nowhere to sleep. Not to mention there were never less than ten people in the house at a time, even if he wasn't home. I thought I could handle it, even talked him into giving me a week, and then the third day happened and I knew it wouldn't last.

I was asleep on the floor in the kitchen, because it was the most private spot in the house. No one ever cooked preferring to stay high. My eyes were closed and I could feel someone taking off my gold bracelets. When I opened them slightly, while still faking sleep, I saw Reds, who Grand called Wet Faye because he claimed her pussy was the juiciest.

Still, was this bitch trying to rob me?

"What the fuck you doing?" I hopped up and pushed her so hard, the back of her bush banged against the stove. A cast-iron pan bopped her on the head before her ass hit the ground. When she was on the floor I rushed toward her but she was quicker and charged at me with clenched fists. When I looked into her eyes I could tell what was up, she was high and deranged.

I was still getting my thoughts together when she brought down her first blow on the side of my temple, and the second on my nose. I wasn't about to go toe to toe with someone on drugs. So I threw my body onto hers, and tackled her to the floor. With her small frame under mine, I pressed my thumbs as hard as I could into her eye sockets. Her fists opened and she scratched at my hands while screaming loudly.

Although the house was full nobody came to help, fighting went on all the time but normally didn't involve me.

I was so tired of the stupid shit that my right thumb pressed a little harder, until blood and white goo splashed on my hand. Scared I had gone too far, I hopped up and looked down at her. She was squirming, screaming and covering her face.

"I can't see!" she yelled bumping around the kitchen. "I can't fucking see! Help me!"

As I looked down I knew my stay at Grand's house was officially over. "I gotta get out of here. He's gonna kill me."

He's finer now than I remembered...

When I ran back into him, the day I poked Wet Faye's right eyeball out, I figured I would be homeless and out on the streets. But after hanging at the bus stop for a few hours, trying to contemplate my next move, he stepped off the bus.

He was dressed to impress and the brown bell-bottoms he wore seemed to flow as he made his way toward my direction. I started to get the impression that the man I saw on the bus that day was drunk because this man looked different, although they were the same.

He stepped so close if he moved too inches more his dick would be in my face. Or as good as he smelled, my mouth. "Thank you, for saving my life." His tone was soft but his gaze was intense as he peered down.

I smiled, too goofy to say much else.

"What you doing?" He looked at the bus and back at me. "You gonna miss your ride."

It pulled off anyway before I could respond. It's a good thing I wasn't waiting. "I'm not here for the bus," I sighed, trying to look more pitiful. "I'm just…waiting…"

He nodded. "You on hard times?"

"Guess you can say that." I shrugged as I looked around him, although I wanted to keep my eyes on his handsome face.

He clasped his hands together in front of him. And although I couldn't see his eyes I knew they were on me. I felt like he was trying to think really hard before deciding to say anything else. As if whatever he said was going to change his life forever.

He released his hands. "I came up on a few bucks." I looked up at him. "Want to get a room?"

That's pretty much how it went down. Not a whole lot of squiring about town or nothing like that. After becoming un-benefit with my mother and squishing my brother's main girlfriend's eyeball out, I was homeless. Luckily for me this time Rufus was in the rescue business.

From the moment I took him up on his offer we were inseparable for an entire week, spending most of our time together in a cramped motel room. But he was funny and catered to me so the days flew by. If I wanted something to eat, no matter the hour he would jump up and get McDonalds. If my body ached and I was uncomfortable he would give me a massage or find some Tylenol. And since I was at his beckon call I was fully prepared to be as freaky as he desired but it didn't go down like that. We made love once, and it was face-to-face, soft and slow. Nothing like I would expect from someone beating his dick on the bus. Maybe he didn't find me that attractive after all.

Humph.

And then there were other times. The occasions that made me shiver when he would sit silently in the room, his chair faced the wall. I made a mistake of touching him on the shoulder once to ask if he was okay during one of these times. He almost broke my fingers, bringing me to my knees. I always wondered where his mind wandered but I learned to leave him be.

Over the days something else happened. I noticed he wore the same outfit, losing his shiny appeal as time went by. But who was I to complain? I was wearing the same shit too.

On the fifth day we were in a small diner, me sitting on Rufus' lap. His hand was under my skirt; his thumb was pressed against my clit as he flicked it back

By T. Styles

and forth. He had an obsession with doing sexual things in public and I was too afraid to ask why. But as I looked around, embarrassed at the people staring our way I knew I needed to say something.

"Rufus, I don't dig this." I grinned.

"Dig what...being with me?"

"No." I smiled down at him. "Being with you in *public.*"

His thumb stopped moving and he pointed at the seat across from him. I quickly sat in my own chair and stared. "Can I ask you something...when we first met you were...you were...satisfying yourself on the bus. Why?"

"No I wasn't." He frowned.

I laughed, thinking he was playing but another look into his eyes told me he was serious. "Rufus, I saw you beating your dick, right before that man killed you and I saved your life," I whispered.

He picked up the menu on the table. "What you want to eat?"

We placed our orders and then silence stood between us for a while. I noticed that his moods were fleeting, never staying the same for longer than an hour.

I put my hands on the table and he placed his on top of mine. I noticed the front of his shirt was speckled with small spots. "You gonna be my wife and have my son." Since he was just trying to fuck me in public I was surprised at his announcement.

"A son huh?" I laughed. "That's kind of specific don't you think, Rufus?"

His smile went away and he released my hand. His personality shifted to something weird again. Not mean, not happy…just weird. "You ever been to Uranus?" His eyes were wide.

With a dropped jaw I said, "I don't know what you mean."

"You ever get so high nothing matters? So high everything in the world is peaceful?"

I shook my head so hard I thought it would twist off. I barely drank alcohol so drugs were out of the question. "I don't fuck around, you know that. Besides I've seen what it does to people."

"Then you a fool." He frowned, slamming his hand on the table. "Dr. King dead. Malcolm X dead. Black people treated like third world citizens in America. How can a man shake it all 'cept he high?"

"That's not my thing that's all," I said softly, scratching my arm. "But more power to you...get high."

He didn't seem appreciative of my statement. His upper lip twitched and when he glanced to his right he saw a black dude with a low cut staring at me. He had been for some time but I tried to ignore him. He seemed business-fied — wearing a navy blue suit with a black briefcase at his feet.

"You got a problem with your looking space, blood?" Rufus asked the man as his fingers crawled into two fists that sat on top of the table, knocking at the wood.

I swallowed my embarrassment and looked down. I wasn't sure but something told me it wouldn't end well.

"Damn, brother," the Businessman said. "If you gotta check every cat who looks at your lady, maybe you don't deserve to have her."

I never saw anybody move as quickly as Rufus. And as long as I lived I hoped to never see anybody fly that quickly again. The rage that hovered over him as he approached the Businessman was strong. He kicked and pounded the stranger like he was trying to kill him, and even took to whipping him over the head with his own briefcase.

Where was this rage with Muscle Man?

When I saw the man's skin open up, his lip bleeding and his cheek swelling, I knew I had to do something. "Rufus, please don't!" I yelled approaching him. I pulled on his shoulders, which were as stiff as a brick wall. "You're gonna kill him!"

"That's the plan, woman!"

When I saw a waitress pick up the phone and make a call I knew it was only a matter of time. I had to act fast or the man would be dead and Rufus in jail. I smacked him so hard Rufus turned toward me, hand open like he was going to hit me back.

"Somebody called the cops, Rufus! Let's go, please."

Rufus blinked a few times, grabbed my hand and pulled me out of the diner. I could hear the police sirens in the air. When we ran outside I knew it was a matter of time before they caught us, besides, we were on foot.

I thought all was lost until he dragged me toward a white man getting ready to step inside a brand new yellow Chevrolet Vega. When the man wasn't looking

Rufus placed his hand under his shirt and approached him like he had a gun. "This a stick up! Give me the keys!"

The White Man's face turned beet red as he tossed the keys to me. Automatically I opened the car door, jumped behind the driver's seat while Rufus slid into the passenger's. It was like second nature. Once things were set into motion I became his bottom bitch as I pulled away from the scene. Through the rearview mirror I could still see the man holding his hands up, except now he had a wet stain on the front of his pants. Maybe he pissed himself.

"Say, baby, you are out of sight!" Rufus said leaning over to kiss me on the cheek. "In a crisis you come through. That makes you a keeper."

Although it was wrong to rob someone if felt like the best day of my life and for some reason I didn't feel one ounce of remorse. I was starting to worry about how much alike we really were. After taking his directions for twenty minutes I was growing agitated because whenever I asked for the destination he kept throwing out orders. "Are you gonna tell me where we going or not?"

"I am telling you, now make a left on that street." He pointed ahead and I followed his lead. Before long we were in front of a set of row homes in Washington D.C. I parked in the first available space and looked around.

"You ready?" he asked rubbing my leg.

"Who lives here?"

He kissed my nose and then my cheek. "Us." He opened his door and I did the same. Quickly, fearing if I didn't I would get left behind, falling into homelessness again.

When he reached the only house on the block with a green door he knocked twice and a chocolate female with hazel eyes and long cornrows running down her back opened it. She was pretty, whoever she was but her attitude was shitty. Her dark skin seemed to glow but her eyes were baggy, like she was stressed. "Where have you been, Rufus?" Her hands seemed magnetized to her hips. "I been looking for you, for weeks!"

He walked in and I followed, closing the door behind myself. She was too young to be his mother so I figured she was an aunt or sister.

Rufus cut the lights off first. "It's too bright in here." He yawned. "I had something to do but I'm home now." He walked into the kitchen, grabbed two beers and handed one to me. Then he kicked off his shoes in the middle of the floor.

As if she finally saw me she looked at him and back at me. "And who the fuck is this?"

Rufus walked toward the back of the house with me on his heels. "My cousin." My stomach dropped and when she turned her head he winked at me. "Bernice, this is my wife Jackie and Jackie this is family." We both walked into a small room and he closed the door in her face.

Inside of the room were a twin size bed and two brown recliners. It looked more like a den with bedroom tendencies. "What was that, Rufus?" I whispered. "The last I remember we had sex. And now we're supposed to be kin?"

He gulped the rest of the beer, tossed a cushion off one of the recliners and removed a plastic bag. I'd been around my brother enough to know heroin when I saw it. Removing the contents, which included cotton, a syringe, a rubber strap and a bent spoon, I watched him do his thing.

"Are you gonna answer me or not?" I placed the beer on the floor and crossed my arms over my breasts. "Because I'm about to leave."

"Listen, you're homeless, baby girl," he tapped the vile a few times, and injected the needle in his arm. "I'm looking out for you, maybe you should be a little more grateful." When he was done he tossed it on the table and looked at me through squinted eyes. His voice slurred as he asked, "Want...want...me to get you right?"

I kicked the beer over, stormed out of the room and then out of the house.

CHAPTER THREE

BERNICE

I was getting some good sleep until my mother woke me up with a smack to the face with the bottom of her dingy flip-flop. "Get the fuck up, lazy!"

I rolled over in the bed, sat up and rubbed my face. "Mama, you don't have to hit me to get attention." I rubbed my cheek.

She dropped the shoe on the floor, slipped her size 10 foot inside of it and closed the first button on her maid uniform, the one closest to her hairy chin. "Don't tell me what I can do. I only let you back because you said you would help me with your father. Now I'm on the way to work and he's in the tub waiting. Get him cleaned up and don't forget to take the chicken out of the freezer."

I sighed. Every thing with her was done with an attitude and a scream. That's one of the reasons I preferred not to be home. I can't remember one day when my mother was happy all day. It's like she blamed me for being born. "Alright, mama." I rubbed my throbbing face again.

"You don't have to if you don't want to, Bernice. I can just call my boss and tell him I need another day to get your father together. It ain't like he won't give it to me."

"You love to fight with me," I said under my breath.

"Why would I fight with you? Huh? You're my child. You're the one who comes in and out of this house mad at us because you wanted a life we couldn't offer. Mad at us because we couldn't buy you fashionable clothes and shoes. Mad at us because—"

"You and daddy were on heroin for most of my life," I said interrupting her.

Her jaw dropped and I knew I went too far.

"You're right, we did make a few mistakes." She stepped closer. "But don't ever think the same thing can't happen to you."

"I will never be on drugs, ma. And I would never abandon my child and leave her to take care of herself like you and daddy did to me."

"You think you so strong, and I hope you are, let's just hope you don't live long enough to eat your own words." Her jaw twitched. "Look, I wasted enough time on you and now I'm late for work. Are you gonna take care of your father or not?"

"I said I got it, ma, just go on." I stood up so she could believe me, grabbed my black robe and walked her into the living room.

When she opened the front door and I heard the car door slam I crawled back into bed for a few more minutes. My father was a grown man. He'd be okay if I caught a few more Z's.

I must've been sleep for about thirty minutes when I heard, "My dick cold! Help me! My dick cold!"

I jumped out of bed and stood in the middle of the room. At first I thought I was hearing things until he called out again.

"My dick cold! My dick cold! Help me!"

Rolling my eyes I sighed, tied my robe tighter and walked into the bathroom. Before doing anything I stood in the doorway and looked at him. There my chubby father was, sitting in the tub looking at me with wide eyes. For the past ten years my father has had severe dementia. Even before then he was moody and would forget things but my mother thought it would go away. It took years for her to understand that it never would.

Although he was out of touch with reality more times than not, he had moments when his thoughts were very clear. Rare moments when he could remember the most interesting stories about his past and I was always intrigued. During those times I loved being around him.

During times like this I didn't.

Feeling bad for dosing back off, the first thing I did was turned the warm water on. Then I grabbed the soap and the yellow washcloth floating in the water. When his bath was the right temperature I turned the water off, made the rag sudsy and cleaned him good. Helping him to his feet I attempted to wipe his penis, which was my least favorite part, but it kept hiding between the sack of his balls. This thing was so small I wondered how he fucked my mother and I was conceived.

"You okay now, daddy? Need anything else?"

"Who are you?"

I smiled and exhaled. "I'm your daughter, don't you remember?"

"You my woman?" He didn't understand a word I was saying.

"No daddy, I'm your daughter."

I kissed him on the cheek and tried to hold back tears. Sometimes I think if my father was well, my mother and me would have a better relationship. I think she resented me for not allowing her life to become my own.

When I was younger, and Grand was still home, I was the one who could never go anywhere. I was the one who had to help mama with daddy. Grand was a boy and mama thought that meant he needed a social life. But where was mine?

It was because of her letting him do anything he wanted that my brother took partying to another level.

It wasn't until last year that I decided not to be my mother's slave anymore and we had been fighting ever since. Sometimes I wished she would stop looking for me and leave me alone when I was out in the streets, but she never did. Grand said it was because she loved me but I didn't believe him.

If anything she hates me and I hate her too.

After my father was clean I helped him out of the tub and he seemed to be relaxed. As if the last outburst never happened. I wrapped him in his blue robe. He was so serene that I thought something was up and then I felt it. It was warm and wet and sat in the middle of my right foot. When I looked down I couldn't believe it, he shitted on me.

"Daddy, what are you doing?" I yelled, kicking my foot to get it off. It plopped on the floor. "Why didn't you tell me you had to go? We were in the bathroom!"

Instead of answering he continued to empty his bowels in the middle of the hallway. I was filled with anger. Why was I back here? I felt my chest wanting to explode and my temples throbbed.

If I stayed this kind of thing would happen all of the time and I'm not sure I could take it. When I looked into his eyes I felt sorry for him because I knew he didn't know what he was doing. Still, it wasn't my fault either and I didn't want this to be my life.

"Stay right here, daddy," I pointed at him. "Do not move."

I left him in the middle of the hallway, grabbed some newspapers from the kitchen and placed them on the floor. I helped my dad down so that his rear was directly on President Nixon's face. "Listen, daddy, I'm gonna leave you here for a second. I'll be back in a—"

When there was a knock at the door my eyes widened and my heart rocked. If my mother doubled back and saw her husband like this it would be the end of my time on earth.

Slowly I walked to the window next to the door, glanced out and saw a yellow Vega outside. Quickly I looked down at myself, took a deep breath and opened the door. There Rufus was, smelling good and looking great. Wearing all black and a gold pinky ring he looked like Marvin Gaye, except he had a baldhead. I was always amazed at how he switched from wretched to impeccable in a second. "What you want?" I asked as if uninterested.

"You."

I sighed. "How you know where my pad was?"

"You told me, when we were drinking at the motel one night. Said you lived on Kennedy, and your crib was the only one with an ugly blue and white awning." He looked up at it and back at me. "Why you leave?" He squinted his nose. "And what's that smell?"

I tucked the foot that my daddy shit on further behind me. "I left because you got me in the same house as your old lady and I didn't even know you had one."

"She's a square, mama. Not down like you." He reached for me and I could smell his cologne. "I'm only staying with her because she got a job at the printing plant, and good benefits. But the plan always been to drop her."

"And that's supposed to make me feel better? You do that to her, how I know you won't do the same to me?"

"Because you in on the secret and she's not. Let her think we just cousins and come back with me. As long as I get to take care of you what difference does it make? You don't want to be here, I know it." He looked over my shoulder and my father had wandered behind me, a piece of newspaper stuck to his ass.

I looked at my dad and shook my head. "Rufus, I got stuff to do."

He laughed, I must didn't sound too convincing. "So what you gonna do now? Live with your mother and be her slave? Come on, babes. This spots no place for a dame like you."

He was weakening me with each word. The more I thought about it the more it made sense. He had to care about me, why else would he bring me in the house with his wife? Besides, if she was stupid enough to believe I was family that was her problem not mine.

"You coming back B? Where I can take care of you and get you right?"

I looked into his eyes. My heart said, 'what are you waiting on', but my mind warned me that something was wrong with this man. When my father walked closer and I could smell him I sighed. "Give me a second. Let me take care of him and I'm leaving...with you."

CHAPTER FOUR

BERNICE

Cops took the Vega the night before, and we had planned to use it to go to the store.

We woke up that morning, planning to buy seafood from the Warf in Washington DC, when we looked outside and it was gone. Realizing the car wouldn't be ours forever, and grateful they didn't catch us in it, I was somewhat relieved. Still, without a ride we were back on the bus, something I wasn't looking forward to with Rufus' weird jerking habit.

I was standing in the middle of the kitchen dicing potatoes and onions for breakfast when Jackie walked up behind me. I looked over my shoulder at her, and noticed she seemed to get prettier as the days passed.

Rufus was 19 and it was hard to understand what he wanted with a 17 year old when he had Jackie who was 22 and had her shit together. She was a total package—beautiful, employed and a homeowner.

Judging by her chocolate skin tone and recalling the woman on the bus, I think he had a thing for darker women. And since I was light skin I was all confused.

"Where is he?" she asked, slinking into the kitchen, wearing a red silk chemise that hugged all of her curves. She was too close and it made me uncomfortable.

Dicing more onions although I didn't need anymore I said, "He went to get fish from the Warf." I glanced at the clock on the wall and back on the food. "He's been gone a little over an hour. Should be back soon."

"How he get there? My car in the shop?"

I shrugged. "Told me not to worry, just to have breakfast ready so that's what I'm doing." I tossed the cleaned diced potatoes in the cast iron pan with the onions, placing a little water and butter inside, just enough to cover the bottom. "Hungry?"

"I think you lying, bitch," she said harshly.

I turned the eye to the stove on calmly, even though my stomach felt like it was in my coody-cat. I covered the pan with the top, turned around and said, "Did you say something?"

"You heard me, and I know you not who you say you are." Her face was tight but the corners of her mouth held a smile. "Are you really his cousin?"

"Jackie, I don't know where all of this is coming from. If you felt like you didn't believe me why you didn't talk to Rufus?"

"Because he's saying the same shit, that ya'll blood. But how come I never saw you before?"

"You know Rufus got a huge scattered family. Most of them down 'Ssissippi."

"Don't you mean most of ya'll down Mississippi?"

Oops.

"Listen, you'd be hard pressed to get all of us in one room together." I sighed but walked toward her as if I meant no harm. "Jackie, I want to like you, I really do, but you gotta stop accusing me of stuff. This the first time you saying something about me living here but I feel tension when you look at me everyday. I am his cousin, but if you want me to leave just say it."

"Why? So I can lose contact with Rufus again? And have him blame me?"

"All the same, it's your call not mine." I threw my hands up in the air and released them.

Silence.

Suddenly I saw the tension disperse from her body, and she seemed lighter. "I'm sorry…it's just that Rufus never gave me any reason to trust him if you know what I mean."

"Then talk to him, but you can't make me uncomfortable because ya'll got a trust issue."

She exhaled, walked up to me and put her arms around me. Her breasts smashed against mine and the hug felt fake. "You right." She released me and looked down at the pan. "That's smelling good already. Can't wait to taste —"

Suddenly I heard screaming followed by loud dog barks outside of the house. When I rushed toward the window I saw Rufus being chased by three black Doberman Pinschers. "Open the fucking door!" he yelled when he spotted me looking out at him. "Now for they kill me!"

I quickly obeyed and he fell into the house, just as one of the dog's noses got caught in the door trying to get inside. I slammed it so hard on the animal that it whined and backed away. The three of us rushed toward the window, Rufus on his knees and watched the dogs circle our porch before running off.

"What the fuck was that?" Jackie asked as Rufus crawled toward the sofa. Sitting on the floor, his back was against the front of the couch, a woman's black leather purse clutched against his chest.

"I don't know what the fuck's up with them dogs." His breaths were heavy and I could sense that he struggled to get himself under control.

"Sure it doesn't have anything to do with that purse in your palm?" she continued. "You robbing women again?"

Robbing women? What was up with this man?

He looked down at it, as if he'd forgotten all about it. "What this?" he raised it in the air and I could tell it was expensive. "This mine." He stood up, walked to his room and came back out empty handed. "Breakfast smells out of sight, cousin. What you cooking?"

I hated that shit but I had to play along.

Rolling my eyes I said, "Potatoes, eggs and bacon. Everything you asked for."

"Well I can't wait to —"

"I don't like that shit," Jackie continued, cutting him off. Her inability to let shit go was one of the things he hated about her. He told me himself. Either she was going to deal with his quirky moods or put him out because in his mind there weren't a lot of options. "Where did them dogs come from?"

He exhaled. "They were with the lady I snatched the purse from."

"Who snatches a purse from someone with big ass dogs?" she asked with wide eyes.

I wanted to know the answer too.

"Let it go, Jackie," he walked around her, toward the refrigerator.

"I'm tired of letting shit go. You get to do whatever you want and who is left to clean things up? Me!" she pointed at herself. "That shit better not fall on my doorstep because you out of —"

He moved quickly again, like the time we were in the diner and he hit that man over the head with his own briefcase. Except now he gripped her neck so tightly I thought for sure he was about to kill her. He looked down at her, his eyes barely visible due to frowning. "I said...let...it...go."

He released her, and she dropped to the floor, knees slamming into the brown carpet. While she hacked for breath he walked up to me, kissed me on the cheek and walked into their marital bedroom.

I didn't see him for the rest of the night.

I ate potatoes and onions all day while Jackie was in the bedroom getting dick.

There in the living room, sitting on the sofa, I stuffed my face and watched the door of their marital bedroom while I listened to her soft moans. My blood felt as if it were bubbling over and my temples throbbed. He was fucking her, and they were loud, and he could care less how I felt.

This was the first time he stayed in her room while I was awake. Normally he'd wait her out until she fell asleep, visit me in my room, fuck my brains out and then go back to her room after I was sound asleep. I guess this was his way of apologizing for choking her so hard she wore a red bruise around her throat like a necklace.

I was about to leave to go anywhere when there was a soft knock at the front door. Taking a deep breath I went to answer it, only to see Otis, Rufus' best friend on the other side.

Otis was about Rufus' age and so handsome it was hard to look at him. His father was Mexican and his mother was black, which made him look Indian. We didn't talk much but when he did I couldn't help smiling. I liked him most of the time but he only visited when he had an idea for trouble and needed Rufus' help.

Working as a groundskeeper, and always coming over straight from work, he brought with him the musk of a man who'd been in the field all day, which I also loved. "Hey, beautiful, where Rufus?"

I pouted and walked toward the couch and flopped down, my arms crossed over my breasts. "In there... with his wife."

"You act like you mad," he said closing the door.

He stood in front of me and I could now smell him better. "Don't play with me, Otis. I know that you are fully aware who I am." I leaned back, trying my best to disappear within the cushions of the sofa.

"Cheer up, I got something for you." He reached into his pocket. "I came to give it to Rufus but since he's tied up he can catch me next go 'round." He removed a bag of light brown heroin and it dangled in front of me. "Want to get right?"

I frowned and pushed his hand away. "You know I don't fuck around with that shit."

His head dropped and he shook it softly. "How you with Rufus and don't get high?"

I lowered my voice, remembering we were louder than we should be. What if Jackie heard us? "You got to ask him that."

He reached into his other pocket and removed a small paper bag. "What about this?" When he pulled a bottle out I saw it was E&J brandy. "Better?"

I smiled. "Yeah, we can start there."

For the next hour Otis and me got pissy drunk. I was doing my best to pretend like I was having the time of my life, hoping that Rufus would come out and get insanely jealous, but he never did. After awhile I could no longer hear Rufus and Jackie, even though I'm sure he was still fucking her. He could go all night and often I had to tap out because I couldn't hang.

Anyway I don't know why it happened, maybe it was the Temptations and Marvin Gaye albums we kept playing, but before I knew it I was sitting on the kitchen sink, legs open as Otis sucked my pussy.

He was good at it too.

So good that I planted one foot on his right shoulder blade and the other on his left. I was in awe as his pink tongue nestled in my asshole; slowly crawling it's way toward the opening of my pussy. Twirling around for a moment he seemed to trip on my clit and that's when he applied pressure. He was sucking, flipping and kissing it so good, I grabbed the back of his head and mashed his face into my sweetness.

And then I said it.

"I want some dick," I whispered.

He jumped up before I had a moment to change my mind and before I knew it I was stuffed, as he gripped the back of my head, nestling my face in the pit of his shoulder blade. He was warm and big and at first I didn't think I could take him but he juiced me up moments earlier. Allowing him to slide inside without a problem. Anyway it was too late because suddenly there was a stream of warm liquid oozing from between my legs.

He had cum inside of me.

That quick.

I didn't even get mine off!

He slipped out of me and looked toward Rufus and Jackie's door and it was still closed. His teeth were clenched as he said, "Why you make me do this to my friend, woman?"

Wait, was he blaming me? "You playing right? I didn't make you do anything."

"This not a joke." He was serious and I wanted to laugh in his face. "You ain't nothing but a jezebel trying to come in between two friends." He zipped up his pants and walked toward the living room.

Embarrassed I hopped off the sink and followed just so I could lock the door, go to my room and cry my eyes out. Before leaving he turned around and looked me in the eyes. "If you tell him about this I'ma kill you," he whispered. "That nigga is crazy and if I have to I'll take the life out of your body myself." He clenched his fists and shook them in my face. "With my bare hands."

CHAPTER FIVE

BERNICE

A few days later we were walking down the street and I still felt guilty for doing Otis in the kitchen. I'd been living with Rufus for two months, while he kept me in a bedroom no bigger than a walk in closet. He fucked his old lady and me as much as he desired and I never said a thing. So why did I feel like the whore? And why was I still dreaming of Otis?

"Rufus, I'm not sure if I can do this anymore." I looked over at him as we passed a cute black couple. She was wearing a yellow mod skirt and white go-go boots and her man was dressed in blue bell-bottom jeans.

They looked happy while we were miserable.

"You must've talked to your mother."

I frowned, not understanding what she had to do with anything. "I talked to her yesterday, on my birthday. But it has nothing to do with us."

He stopped walking and looked surprised. "You turned 18 already?"

I frowned. "You don't remember me reminding you? And you telling me it was just another day when I cried because my mother told me to fuck off. Because she's still mad I left my father alone when I came back to you."

He waved me off. "Later for all that. I wanted to talk to you about something else. He grabbed my hand and pulled me toward him, like I was a kid who didn't know how to walk down the street alone. "She's getting suspicious." He dropped is arm around my neck like a weight as we moved down the block, toward a park. It felt heavy, like he was bearing all of his weight on purpose.

"Don't know how she could, you do what you want when you want. I hardly see you." My heart felt like it was shrinking as I realized if I stayed with him my life would get worse. I had to find a way out.

"Listen at you," he laughed.

"I'm serious, Rufus. What am I doing in her house if you not making future plans with me? Seems like you having everything you want at once."

"That's how it should be. I'm a man and you don't get to say how things go down in this relationship. And the moment you think you do I will be forced to straighten you out. And trust me." He grinned widely. "You don't want that."

I stepped away and he yanked me back, throwing his arm around my shoulder again as we moved toward a trail within the park. Rufus's moods shifted so much that it was hard to know when to avoid him. But I also realized I was tired of trying to figure him. So my only plan was to get a job, move and go my own way.

The bouts of him sitting in the corner staring at the wall had also increased and he grew creepier. Over time Jackie and me learned to just leave him alone, knowing he'd be back to himself in a few hours. When I asked her was he like this always she said, "You his cousin, shouldn't you already know?"

I never asked her again.

One of the reasons I called home on my birthday was one, so that I could see if my mother was still mad at me, which she was, and two, to see if I had a chance of coming home, which I didn't. So for now, even though he scared me I was stuck.

"All I know is we got to be careful, Bernice. Do a little more to get to know her."

My neck started to throb and I wiggled a little so he could get off of me but he didn't budge. "You know, maybe we shouldn't fuck no more. It's her pad and since I'm causing strife I'm good with falling back a little."

"You mean as in if I break your jaw fall back?" He seemed alert as he waited for my response, but I didn't give him one.

Instead I swallowed the lump in my throat.

"Falling back ain't no option, Berny. I'm fucking you when and how I want. I'm just suggesting that you play nicer with her, that's all." Suddenly he pushed me in the grass and threw his body on top of me. "Let me feel that pussy right quick."

I tried to wiggle from up under him and at the same time understand what was going on. He was worse than moody, he was insane. "Rufus, I'm not going to do this out here! Get off of me, please!"

"Shut up, you like it like this." I heard the zipper of his pants go down as he pushed my thighs apart. His eyes were wild and he looked like the same man on the bus when I first met him. My mother always said I saw what I wanted when I met a man, and now I understood she was right.

He ripped my panties and spread my vagina lips apart, scratching at my inner walls. "Rufus, please stop! I'm begging you." I didn't want to face it but things were clear, he was about to rape me. He plunged his penis inside of me and his wet lips sat against my earlobe. I thought he was going to bite me. His heavy breaths sounded repulsive and he said a few words that I couldn't make out.

"Damn...this pussy is just right," He moaned.

The more weight he bared down on me the harder it was to breathe. "Rufus, you're hurting —"

In mid conversation a bee floated in my face, flew into my mouth and stung me on the inside of my left cheek. "It stung me! It fucking stung me! Help!" Since I'm allergic to bees, I must've gotten super human strength because I finally managed to push him off.

I got a few steps away when I felt my throat closing.

And then I couldn't breathe, falling face first to the ground.

When I woke up I was lying in the hospital bed and the first nigga I saw was the rapist. He was leaning against the wall, arms crossed tightly over his chest like he was wearing a straight jacket. "You know you pregnant right?" He scratched his chocolate baldhead.

Since I knew I just fucked Otis I was relieved that it couldn't be his. "I don't feel pregnant." I placed my hand on my belly and closed my eyes, trying to sense the life inside of me. When I reopened them he was in my face, hot breath slapping me against the forehead.

"Bitch, I'm telling you what the honkey doctor just told me!" He pointed toward the door. "I'm too young to be having a kid."

"Well I don't believe them, I think it's a mistake." My voice was low.

"Don't be jiving me, Bernice!" He held his elbows wide from his body and his chest thrust outward. "I don't like being fucked with."

I sat up in the bed, trying to think of what to say that wouldn't piss him off. I heard about people being pregnant before and all of them had morning sickness. A few girls on my block had to be hospitalized because they were so bad. It didn't make much sense to me because I couldn't feel no baby in my belly. "Rufus, if

I'm pregnant, if it's true, it ain't just my fault. I didn't fuck myself."

"Don't matter if you did or didn't. Why you don't know how to drop the nut out? Bitches who don't want kids drop the nut, so they can't get pregnant. You should've done the same thing."

Drop the nut? What was he talking about?

His chin rose high and I could see clear into his nostrils. "I can't have no children, Bernice. It's important for you to understand this."

I scratched my scalp, still confused by the rape in the park and now this. It was too much. "At the diner, weren't you the one who said I would have your child?"

"I don't know what you talking about, all I know is you can't have no kids by me. My wife would kill me."

Now she's your wife.

The more I looked at him the more I agreed. Any children born of this fool was bound to be psycho. "You're right, we can't have a baby, now what? Because the last thing I remember was almost dying from a bee sting while you tried to rape me. This is the last thing I need right now."

He rolled up the sleeves to his shirt. "You can't rape what belongs to you." I'm convinced this man is bananas. "Don't worry about nothing." He smiled awkwardly. "I know a woman who can get it out for $250.00. I'm gonna get the money, you just get ready, 'cause I hear it's the most painful thing you'll ever experience."

Later that day, after being discharged from the hospital, I was sitting in the waiting room waiting on Rufus to pick me up. I guess he would use his feet since he didn't have a car and Jackie was at work. All I know was he told me to stay put or we would fight.

I thought about the baby in my stomach, and although I never considered having a kid of my own, I was feeling resentment that he wanted me to throw it away like trash. But I didn't have a place to go and I was slowed up enough as is having to take care of myself. A baby wouldn't fit into my plans.

Holding the purse Rufus lifted off some woman the day the dogs got after him, I patiently waited for him to arrive. One hour turned into two, and after awhile I'd been there so long people were starting to look at me strangely.

I drifted off into a soft sleep when Jackie popped up, face tight with attitude as usual. One side of her hair was braided and the other wasn't, which meant there was trouble in the Miller family again. "I heard you needed a ride."

I was confused. How did she know I was here? Did she know about my baby too? I stood up. "Yeah…I was waiting on Rufus."

"Well you gonna be waiting a long time for that nigga," she said with an attitude and a long eye roll. "They nabbed him for stealing that white woman's purse you holding."

I felt flushed.

I looked at the floor, trying to stop the dizziness. "So…what's gonna happen?"

"What's gonna happen is that his ass is gonna do five years, if not more." She paused. "These whities not playing with niggas out here. Even one that's bipolar like my husband." She shook her head and it was news to me that he had a mental illness even though it explained everything.

"This is so…so crazy." I scratched my bushy hair.

With lowered brows she said, "Rufus told me you were here from an allergic reaction to a bee sting." She paused and looked dead into my eyes. "Ain't nothing else going on is it? Because you can be homeless now, and if I even think something else is up I'm throwing you out on the street! You got that, cousin?"

CHAPTER SIX

BERNICE

I'm in the bed; a month after Rufus was locked up for robbery, wondering why I'm still living in this woman's house. She hasn't said anything foul, but her silence makes me just as uncomfortable. Each day, the baby inside of me grows and I know soon I'll have to explain.

And when I do where will I go?

I didn't go to the hearing but Jackie said Rufus was given a harsh sentence. The judge who presided over his case said he was tired of seeing his name on his dockets and it was time to make him pay. That if Rufus wanted to be in jail he would finally fulfill his wishes and give him ten, with the possibility of parole.

When I turned over in bed, I glanced at the clock. It's 1:00 am and I hear soft sniffling outside of my bedroom. In the past Jackie cried herself to sleep but it was once a week. Now it seemed like every night.

Bored with myself I sat on the side of the bed, planted my toes in the shag carpet and stood up. With a hand on my small belly I exhaled deeply and walked out of the room.

At first I was going to the kitchen, maybe to get a drink but for some reason I felt magnetized to her room, surprising myself when I knocked on the door. "Jackie," I said softly, my forehead against the cool wooden door like a lover who had been thrown out. "Are you okay?"

Silence.

"Please...come...come inside."

I opened the door, preparing to walk back out when I saw that she was lying in a t-shirt on her side, no panties. Her gaze was in the opposite direction. Her hair, which is normally kept in long cornrows running down her back, are still unraveled on one side, falling into crinkly cascades.

"Are you okay?" I rubbed my belly again and stopped when I realized I wasn't supposed to be pregnant, and definitely not by her husband. "Can I get you anything? Something to eat or drink?"

"This is going to sound weird," she said softly, rolling over, her sad eyes looking my way for help. "But can you hold me?"

Before I know it I'm in the bed, my body behind hers with my hand on her warm thigh. I think I needed this more than she did, which is why I moved so quickly. Sometimes the touch of another is better than medicine. Here we were, two women whose lives were torn apart by the same man. "I'm sorry, Jackie, about all of this."

"It's not your fault," she sighed. "I've known him all of my life. Got with him after high school and we've been together ever since. And I know he's selfish, and leaves me for months at a time, but I was always comforted knowing that if I just held on he would return." Her body trembled as she cried a little harder. "I've never been with another man in my life."

I didn't believe her.

But before Otis I could say the same, and now I feel worse about being here. Maybe Jackie was cool and didn't deserve to get hurt, definitely not by the other woman. "Do you think he gonna do the whole ten?"

"Not sure," she shrugged as she rested her hand on top of mine. "Just know that we have to take care of each other now. My family stopped dealing with me after I got with Rufus. Said he was mentally unprepared for life and that I should leave him alone. I could never do it so they cut me off."

My eyebrows rose. "So you want me to stay, in your house?"

"I *need* you to stay," she replied, before drifting into a hard snore filled sleep.

My homemade breakfast potatoes were done and sitting on the table in a red ceramic bowl. The bacon was in the oven and I whipped up some blueberry biscuits that I planned to trickle with warm brown sugar butter when they were out the oven. I was humming a Marvin Gaye song while stirring eggs heavy with cheese, when a warm sensation flooded my belly, rising up toward my throat.

It was morning sickness.

Something I never had before.

Just as I was about to turn and run to the bathroom Jackie came up behind me. Her chin rested on my shoulder as she looked into the bowl. It felt awkward, like we were lovers. "I don't know what I would do without you." She seemed happy while secretly my mouth filled with vomit. All I wanted her to do was go back into the room so I could rush to the bathroom. I couldn't even speak because she would know that something was in my mouth.

And how could I explain sickness?

"You hear me?" she asked.

I nodded.

"So you not talking this morning, grumpy?" she giggled as I heard her feet scurry across the kitchen floor. At least she was away from me. "That's fine, as good as this breakfast smells you can be as quiet as you want." When I heard the refrigerator open my jaw relaxed and vomit slapped into the egg bowl.

I was just about to toss it into the sink when she said, "I'm gonna do the eggs. You don't make 'em cheesy enough for me." She had a block of cheddar in her hand and bumped me softly with her hips. "Go check on the biscuits."

"I don't think I like this batch," I said softly. "The eggs smell bad."

"Girl, I bought these the other day. Just check on the biscuits."

I stood behind her, watching her pepper up the eggs and add more cheese, which eventually concealed my throw up even more. Not being able to hold back anymore, I ran to the bathroom and finished releasing the contents of my gut in the toilet.

I was four or five months pregnant, my belly was getting larger and the morning sickness all gone. The only thing I had to worry about now was Jackie and the constant attention she desired. I started to think that eating those eggs mixed with my bodily contents did some kind of voodoo thing on her. She seemed obsessed with me.

I slept with her so much that she was no longer use to sleeping by herself, even though most nights I wished she would. Sometimes I would lie on my left side and she would spoon me, which was cool until her hand rested on my growing belly one night. "Whoa, mama, getting big ain't you?"

My eyes widened as I tried desperately to think of a lie. I could feel sweat forming around my hairline, my breath quickening and my heart pumping. I would have to tell her I was pregnant and pray she would believe it was by a stranger. And then I heard her snoring.

I was off the hook.

For now.

Rufus called a lot and talked to Jackie but I wasn't allowed to answer the phone. The few times he wanted to speak to me I pretended to be in the bathroom or busy. My loyalty was with Jackie now and I didn't want to disrespect by talking to him. It didn't stop him from trying to reach me although he never could. These days it was about my baby and me.

I was focused.

As the weeks went by something else happened. Otis came over more; he said it was to check on us for Rufus. But I knew that was a lie. If the night ran long during his visits, we would wait Jackie out and sneak in a suck. One thing I liked about Otis was that he loved to eat pussy and would often jerk his dick as he licked me clean. His attention relaxed my spirits and I convinced him that flipping my clit was not doing his friend wrong. Because at least we weren't having sex.

While his lips were pressed against my clit I would say stuff like, "You are such a good friend." *Moan.* "This is so much better. And don't worry, Rufus wouldn't mind and I'll never tell." *Moan. Moan.* "Ummm, keep it right there."

He seemed to want to please me and since I was pregnant with a child nobody knew about but Rufus, I welcomed his attention and touch. I was lonely and sleeping in the bed every night with Jackie was only good for warmth, but I wasn't into women. And as far as I knew she wasn't either.

His private lick sessions went on for days until one night, while lying in bed with Jackie I noticed she seemed restless. She shifted a lot, pulled the covers off of me, forcing me on the cool side of the bed alone. I didn't know what was wrong but felt something was off. And then she said, "You fucking Otis ain't you?"

I nodded yes in the darkness, not sure if she could see me.

"I know you're his cousin but Rufus wouldn't like it, with Otis being married and all. Maybe you should stop it."

Otis is married?

I swallowed the lump. The last thing I needed was her telling Rufus about me and Otis. "Then maybe we shouldn't tell him, Jackie," I said softly. "With him being locked up and all, no sense in making his days longer."

She was quiet and I could hear my own heartbeat in my eardrums. Would she keep my secret? Suddenly I felt her kiss me on the back of my shoulder. "You're so funny, Bernice. That's what I love about you. Always willing to do what's right for family." She exhaled and covered my cold body with the sheet again. "So glad you're here."

Crazy bitch.

I didn't stop being with Otis, just got more creative in how we saw each other. He was still allowed to stop by, so on those days he would fix her favorite drink — Harvey Wallbanger. A mixture of vodka, orange juice and Galliano, it always put her out after two drinks.

As the days crept by the only things that changed was the size of my belly and Jackie's attitude. For some reason she took to spoiling me rotten, buying me new clothes, getting my hair done and even giving me money. I wasn't sure if Rufus told her to be generous but I had a feeling that Jackie didn't do anything she didn't want.

I was showing so much now it was hard to buy baggy clothing big enough to hide my pregnancy. As I showered one day, and looked down, I noticed I could only see the tip of my big toes.

It was settled, I could no longer share Jackie's bed.

On the night I made my decision I cleaned up the kitchen and decided to watch TV. Wearing the biggest sweatshirt I could find I tried to wait her out. It worked until about one o'clock in the morning. I was dozing off when she came out of her room, rubbing her eyes and yawning. "Cut the TV off, Bernice. I need you in bed."

I continued to look at the TV, didn't even bother to gaze her way. "I was thinking of staying up tonight." I fluffed a pillow next to me. "Gonna watch Benny Hill."

She laughed. "Well watch it in my room, silly."

"You don't like the TV on while you're sleeping."

She looked dead into my eyes and it was obvious she was no longer tired. "I'll make an exception, now come to bed."

This isn't going to work. I have to get her use to not sleeping with me. "Jackie, please don't be mad, but I'm gonna stay up and go to bed in my room. I think you need your space and I do too." I smiled, realizing I looked dumb. "I hope you understand."

Her body erected and her expression was cold. "So you don't like sleeping with me? When you know how much I need you?"

I shrugged. "Just for a few nights that's all."

Yeah, until after I have this baby.

"I know you pregnant, Bernice," she said with an attitude. It was like she could read my mind. "But what I don't know is how you gonna tell Otis."

"What...what you talking about?"

"No use in lying. I had a feeling you were fucking him when Rufus was home, just didn't say anything because Rufus can get bananas over the craziest things. You carrying his baby and anybody can see it." She paused. "Now don't make me wait...come to bed or get out of my house!" She turned around, pushed the door open and walked inside.

It looked like she entered the black abyss.

I wasn't feeling this bitch coming at me hard. So for two minutes I thought about my options. I was done being a sucker and it was time I lived my life for me.

It didn't take me long to remember that I was eighteen and unwanted. Where was I going to go? So I found myself cuddling against her sleeping body, a gut full of her husband's baby rubbing against her back.

After days of cuddling and being Jackie's personal toy, I was glad when she had to work the night shift. Some major publisher needed printed books and she was responsible for managing her team to ensure the quota was met.

While she was out I prepared a big dinner for Otis. There was steak, mashed taters and kale greens. The moment he came inside, smelling like he'd been at work all day, my pussy tingled.

As he ate his food, I looked over at him, a huge smile dressing my face. For a moment I imagined he was mine and this was our life. Our house. Our marriage. A strange thing was happening, I found myself falling for him even though we could never be together.

"Why you staring over here, mama?" he winked. "Want some dick or somethin'?"

"You always do know what to say to me."

"I know what that pussy like too."

I smiled and then allowed it to disappear. Swallowing I took a deep breath. "I'm pregnant, Otis," I blurted out. "Have been for some time now."

He placed the fork down. "Go on."

"Now I don't expect you to take care of — "

Otis broke out into laughter and it scared the hell out of me. What was funny about the baby I was trying to put off on him? "I started to let you finish but let me stop you now because I can't take it." He laughed so hard he was tearing up. "Bernice, I'm not able to have kids, woman."

I frowned. "You a man. Why not?"

"Got hit in the penis with a bat at twelve, fucked up some of my internal organs."

I imagined how that was possible but my brain was too foggy.

"And anyway, Rufus told me he planted that spawn months ago. So no need in putting it off on me."

My eyes widened. "But...I...uh..." I was trying to clean up my lie but finding it impossible. The only reason I thought about saying he was the father was so that Jackie wouldn't put me on the streets. I hadn't counted on Rufus telling his best friend about the pregnancy. Besides, Otis never said anything despite all the time we spent together.

"Don't be so surprised," he continued tearing into his steak. "I know why you wanted me to be the father." He talked with his mouth full of meat. "And because that pussy so sweet I'll go along with it for the mean time. After tonight you can tell Jackie it's mine. I'm okay with it."

I was relieved and embarrassed all together. The guilt of what I was about to do, by lying and saying it was his baby, weighed on me. And still he was so calm.

When he finished eating he walked over to me, pulled and tugged my chair so that it was pointed outward, toward him. Once in front of me he dropped to his knees and raised my skirt. "Never lie to me or do something you know could ruin my life. If you do I'll never talk to you again."

I felt a sense of loss already.

Before I knew it he was sucking on my clit, getting it juiced up. My hands ran through his silky hair and all my troubles were over as he licked and flipped my pussy until I had an orgasm. When I was done he stood up and looked down at me. "Stand up, turn around and put your hands on the table."

Feeling too dumb to do anything else, I obeyed. The next minute I was stuffed with dick from the back. I guess we were off the *pussy eating only* tip, and I was thankful because I needed him. I had the feeling that even though he had a wife, he needed me too.

He never talked about her much. I'm not even sure if they're happy. All I know is that when we are together nothing else matters.

His cool hands remained on my hips as I received his dick massage. "This gonna work out just fine, girl. Wait and see."

CHAPTER SEVEN

BERNICE

As the weather got cold, and snow piled up outside, I noticed Jackie got meaner.

Throughout the summer she was easy going and spoiled me so much I wondered was God finally giving me a break due to being born to awful parents. I don't feel that way anymore. It's like she knows that with the weather being bad she can treat me however she wants and what could I do?

I'm totally depended on her.

It was pitch black in the room. I was lying in her bed, my back faced against her back, It was too hard to spoon these days because being nine months pregnant meant my hard belly was pressed against her back, which irritated her. But still she wanted me in her bed, if nothing else for body warmth.

I was just about to dose off when I heard a squishy noise. At first the noise was soft and then it got louder, and was followed by her moaning. As the bed rocked lightly I finally understood what was happening. This nasty bitch was fingering her pussy.

With me next to her.

I didn't mind holding her, because most nights I needed the connection myself, but I wasn't into girls and would never be. Before now she never did anything like this and I was hoping she never would again.

Suddenly I heard her moan louder. It was heavier than the last sound so I figured she must've came. I was hoping she went to sleep but instead she turned around and placed her hand on my thigh.

Her fingers were creamy wet and it made my skin crawl.

I screamed inside.

I was about to get out of the bed thinking she wanted something else, instead she drifted off to sleep.

Otis came over the next day and shoveled snow out of the walkway. He and Jackie had been trying to get in contact with Rufus for days and were unsuccessful. When they called the prison they said no information could be given and Jackie made plans to go there next week to find out what was up in person.

I didn't think about Rufus much. Otis gave me the attention I needed and when Jackie was around he played up our lie, that the baby was his and he couldn't wait for it to come. Several times I thought I saw a hint of jealousy in her eyes as he doted over me. I think she wanted me to be alone and totally dependent, but he made it known that he liked my company although I didn't understand why. We all agreed that Rufus couldn't know about Otis and me but to tell you the truth I didn't care if he did.

With Otis in my corner I was cool.

After enjoying hot dogs, fries and cold sodas we were all sitting on the sofa watching TV. I was lying on Otis, my head in his lap as he softly stroked my belly. I could feel Jackie's prying eyes on me but I avoided them, doing all I could to dodge an argument. Sometimes she would make up things to fight about and I didn't have the energy anymore.

Suddenly Jackie sat up and looked at Otis. "Ain't you got to get home to your wife?"

My eyes widened because she never came at him so hard in the past.

"Damn, mama...why you rushing me out?" His eyes were still on the TV and his fingertips still cruising along the length of my pregnant belly. "You know I go home when I'm ready."

She stood up, stomped toward her room and slammed the door. This time we both looked in the direction she walked. "What's up with her?" I said, mostly to myself. "She been acting funky lately."

He coughed, covered his mouth with the hand that touched me and rubbed my belly again. "She fuck you yet?"

I sat up and looked over at him. "*Fuck me?*" I repeated. "What you talking about, Otis?"

He laughed. "Don't get me wrong, Jackie loves dick but she has a passion for pussy. Always has. And if you giving it to her she gonna be hooked and that's when your real problems will begin." He gazed into my eyes. "Hold up, you really didn't know?"

I shook my head.

"Wow, I would've thought Rufus told you that before you moved here. If nothing else so you could be on the look out."

"I...I don't understand."

"Me and Rufus met her while we were in middle school. She was in high school. But the three of us were best friends. She was dealing with Samantha, a lesbian who used to beat her ass. After Jackie got out of high school, she and Samantha bought this house together. We thought things were cool in their relationship until Jackie called us one night and said Samantha had broken her nose."

He stopped talking but I hadn't gotten all of my answers. "So what happened after that?"

"We took Samantha with us to stop them from fighting. Rufus dropped me off home and Samantha went with him. Let's just say nobody ever saw her again and a few months later, when he turned 18, Rufus and Jackie were married."

The hairs on the back of my neck rose. "Did he kill her? Samantha?"

He looked at me for a moment, not saying anything. "Don't fuck with Jackie. Don't let her touch you either. That's a warning."

I wanted more on Samantha but I could tell it wasn't going to happen. "You don't have to tell me not to sleep with her, I don't go that way. With women I mean."

He smiled. When I glanced down at his pants I noticed his dick was stiff. What was up with the people in this house? Everybody seemed to get horny for the strangest things.

Now that I think about it, me too.

"Now we got a situation I need you to take care of." He looked down at his crouch, snaked is fingers through his pants and whipped out his dick. "Come here and fix it."

I was always scared to have sex this far long. Not only was Otis' dick huge but I was also worried he'd hurt the baby. That is until I remembered he was always so gentle. Even making sure I reached and orgasm too. Telling me it was good for shaping the baby's cranium.

When I straddled him, he eased into me and I exhaled. He looked into my eyes like he wanted to say something else. Instead, two pumps later, he splashed his cum into my body and for some reason I felt wetter than usual.

After I had an orgasm, he walked to the bathroom and I lied on my back, knees on the couch, staring up at the ceiling. Otis returned with my warm washcloth and softly wiped my pussy clean. From between my legs he looked like a doctor giving me a strange exam. Tossing the rag on the table he placed his hand on my knee. "You okay?"

I nodded yes.

"I only want the best for you."

"I know," I smiled.

"Let me get out of this bitch's house before I say something I don't mean." He exhaled. "She seems like she's going to be a handful tonight, be careful."

I sat up and suddenly felt a soft pressure on the bottom of my belly. "I think something is wrong."

He leaned forward, kissed me on the forehead and smiled. "Next time I'll take it easier." He stood up. "Probably not a good idea to do it like that no more anyway. It's just that your pussy be so juicy and tight these days."

Was it a swimming pool before?

He grabbed his keys off the end table and walked toward the door. As he opened it I noticed snow covered everything outside. The cold temperature was bone chilling and I couldn't wait for him to close the door. "Damn, I hope you don't have that baby tonight because you'd be in trouble." He walked out and I was warm again.

When the house phone rang I answered, surprised to hear Rufus' voice. I remembered I wasn't supposed to pick up the phone but it was too late. "Now I catch you."

I rubbed my belly. This bitch is going to be mad. "Been busy I guess."

"Too busy to talk to your cousin?"

I smiled, although I wasn't sure why. "Where you been? Jackie and Otis been trying to reach you all night."

"I am where I am," he joked. "Where's Jackie?"

"Right here," she said on the other line. I didn't know she picked up and it's a good thing we didn't say much.

I hung up and walked toward the sofa, my stomach pain getting worse. It wasn't terribly painful. More like I had to poop but when I tried I couldn't. Instead I sat on the sofa for fifteen minutes until I remembered what Otis said. Was I going into labor? I rushed to the window by the door, staring outside I saw how deep the snow had gotten. I just hoped it wouldn't be a problem for the ambulance to get through if it was time to deliver.

Worried, I walked toward Jackie's room. I could hear her laughing, probably talking to Rufus. I opened the door. "I think I'm in labor," I whispered.

There was a reason for my soft voice. There were so many legs to the lie that it was hard to keep track of them all. Jackie believed that Rufus wasn't supposed to know I was pregnant, definitely by Otis. Rufus wasn't supposed to know I was fucking Otis either, which was true. Then there was the truth. Rufus knew I was pregnant because it was his baby, but Jackie didn't know.

She lowered the handset from her ear. "What you say?"

I know she heard me. "I'm having the baby," I whispered again.

She exhaled. "Better call 911."

"I can't...you on the phone."

She sighed, rolled her eyes and said, "I have to go, if you can, call me later. Okay?"

I'm not sure what he said when she hung up and she didn't bother to tell me either. "What I tell you about answering the phone?"

"I forgot."

"Maybe if you didn't fuck so much around here your brain would be clearer." She paused. "The phone is all yours...make it quick."

I rushed into the living room and dialed 911. The pains were more intense and I was starting to worry. "I'm having a baby, I need help." I told the operator, giving her the address.

"We'll get someone out there as soon as we can," the operator replied, her attitude non-chalant.

My eyes widened. "You don't understand, I need help now."

"I get that, but you should also be aware, like I'm sure you are, that we're in the middle of a blizzard. It will take a while for someone to get to you. Now I really am sorry but it's all I can do."

Now what?

After hanging up I flopped on the sofa. My breaths were heavy and I wasn't sure if it was a pregnancy symptom or my nerves. I didn't feel much better when she came out of her room, arms crossed over her chest. "I know you don't think you about to have no slimy baby on my sofa."

With wide eyes I said, "Exactly where do you want me to have it? I called 911 and they don't know when they'll get here."

She rolled her eyes, stormed into her bedroom and slammed the door.

I'm so sick of that bitch I could scream. Any other time I could take her mood swings but now I was about to have a baby. And since it didn't look like she was going to help me, it would be alone.

The first thing I did was slowed down my breaths. "You can do this, Bernice. You're going to be okay. Just remain calm." I chanted those words repeatedly until I could feel myself relaxing. I knew I had to have this baby no matter what so I couldn't make things worse by being upset.

I was about to go sit in a tub of warm water when Jackie stormed back into the living room. She tossed the winter coat she just bought me in my face. One of the buttons scratched my nose. "You gotta get out of here. You can't be having no babies in my house."

I stood up, and caressed my belly, not sure if it was for pity or pain. "Jackie, please don't do this. I don't have anywhere to go tonight. You know that. Look outside, I'll die out there."

She stomped past me and opened the door. Snow flurries floated inside and dusted the place where she stood, even her toes. "Don't like your attitude and it's not my problem." She pointed outside. "Get out."

Sliding the coat on, as slowly as possible, I hoped she changed her mind. Hoped she'd laugh and cry joking. Grabbing my black boots by the door I slid them on one by one, still she was waiting for me to leave. "Jackie, you can't do this."

Silence.

"I'll die out there, my baby too," I pleaded.

"I'm cold, you gotta leave." She shivered.

What did she think would happen to me?

I felt like I was in an awful dream, one that wouldn't end well. Obeying her wishes I stepped out of the house and turned around to face her. I thought I saw a smirk and felt in my heart she wanted me to beg. I would if I had the energy but I didn't.

So she slammed the door.

I turned around and faced the city. There was no color. Everything was white. It felt like the world was toppling down around me and I would cry, except my teardrops would freeze. The pain in my stomach was so great now I had to sit on the top step. The door was at my back, the snow so deep it covered the sides of my legs. I thought all was lost until I saw a truck with a snow plow in front of it.

I blinked a few times when I saw Rufus' face in the driver's seat. I stood up preparing to run to him until I passed out, face first into the snow.

I gave birth to a baby boy, his warm body was nestled against my breasts as I looked down at him. The doctors and nurses all smiled at me but my focus floated to other thoughts.

How was this possible?

He was the most beautiful thing in the world and I didn't have a thing to offer. Just because I am his mother, he would have a hard life.

I kissed his forehead.

"What's his name?" a white nurse asked, with a smile so large it took up the bottom half of her face.

By T. Styles

The first name I thought about was Kaden but I knew a dude who raped girls with that name, which is probably why it stuck in my head. Then I thought about Rufus but that was just plain ugly.

"Ka...Ka...Ka..." my tongue flapped around because whatever name I chose he would be stuck with for life. Some people throw out names without thinking but since I couldn't give him money, I wanted his name to be something he'd be proud of.

"Ka?" The nurse repeated. "How are you spelling that?" She frowned.

I looked down at him again and said, "Ka...Ka..." My thoughts floated again. Suddenly I was thinking about how if the stranger driving down the street, the one with the snowplow, that I thought was Rufus hadn't stopped, neither of us would've survived.

My baby would not have *lived*.

"Did you say *live*?" The nurse asked again. I didn't know I verbalized my thought and she was growing agitated.

"Mam, I'm not understanding...you said Ka and live. Which one is his name?"

I looked up at her again. "Kalive..." I smiled. "I'll call him Kalive. Kalive Davenport."

CHAPTER EIGHT

BERNICE

Kalive was a month old as I lie on a clean pallet on my brother's floor in his living room. A chubby baby, his legs and arms looked like a pile of tires. I didn't bother asking Jackie if I could stay with her, since she let her feelings be known by throwing me outside during the dead of winter while in labor. But Grand also made it clear that he wasn't feeling his grove being stunted by his little sister and her baby either.

"You can't stay here long, Bernice. You gotta start taking care of yourself." He told me as he rolled reefer into a joint while sitting on the edge of his bed. "This no place for a kid and I don't want you getting comfortable."

"You always judging me but what about your son? The one you don't claim?"

Why did I just do that? I'd known about my nephew Vaughn for a while but never said anything out loud.

By T. Styles

He looked away. "Ain't no proof he's my kid but if there is I'll do right by mine. Don't worry about that, let's talk about you."

"I'm sorry."

"Fuck sorry, Bernice. Like I said before don't get comfortable here. Plus Wet Faye still mad at you for poking her eye out. And if I'm being honest, I'm mad too. She was a pretty something before you ruined her."

I frowned, and rocked my baby a little harder out of nervousness. I slowed down when he spit up and it splashed against my breast. "She stays here? Still?"

"In jail now for fighting some white woman at a civil rights march on the Monument. Should be home any day now, when I can put the money to the side to get her out." He lit his reefer, pulled and blew out smoke.

I covered Kalive's nose.

"You're my brother, Grand. Mama not answering her door and I don't got no place to be. So I want to know what you saying?"

"What I'm getting at is that leaves you with five days tops to get you some other business." He pointed at me with the joint. "Use each one wisely, dig?"

And I did.

The first thing I knew that I had to do was find a gig. Luckily one of the girls who stayed with Grand had a thing for babies. Hers was taken some months back because like me, she didn't have a place to go. She agreed to help so I could find a job so the same thing wouldn't happen to me.

With her watching Kalive, during the day I searched for employment. I knew she was a junkie but whenever I came home Kalive was clean and fed and since I didn't have help, as a beggar I couldn't choose.

Nobody minded holding Kalive because he was a respectful baby, only crying when he was wet or hungry. I joked to Grand that he was probably saving his voice for the hell he would raise when he got older. Considering his father was crazy we both agreed it wasn't funny, for fear my words might turn to reality.

Three days later I had been out all day trying to find a job and when I walked through the front door I saw Wet Faye standing in the living room, my son nestled under her left breast.

She was out of jail.

With outstretched hands I walked carefully toward her, as humble as possible. I would've gotten

By T. Styles

on my knees if there weren't so much trash on the floor. "Faye, I'm begging you, please don't hurt my baby."

She smiled in a way only an evil person could, when they were aware they had their victim right where they wanted. There was an eye patch over the missing eye, which made her look sinister. "What you doing here, Bernice?" She addressed me but her gaze was on Kalive's sleeping face. "Huh? Didn't I tell you not to come 'round here again?" Now she focused on me and I shivered.

"I wasn't gonna stay long. Grand gave me five days and I've been working hard to find a place of my own. But if you give me my son I'll leave today...right now."

She smiled again. "What if I told you it was too late?" She held Kalive upside down by his left leg before tossing him a few feet away. I thought I was going to die as I watched him flying through the air, his arms held tightly against his body.

Kalive landed on his back, on a pile of clothes and I'd never been so happy in my life. His wide eyes looked around, probably wondering what was happening.

With him no longer in her clutches I leapt toward her, this time with plans to choke her until the life drained from her body. On top of her, I slapped and clawed at her face, the patch she wore lied next to her head revealing a cream color hole.

I was able to get my fingers around her neck, and was about to squeeze when she slapped me on the side of the face with a glass ashtray. I picked up one of the shards preparing to cut her throat when I was suddenly whisked up by the back of my shirt and flung across the room, not too far from Kalive.

It was Grand.

He was breathing heavily as he looked over at me and I knew I'd gone too far. Once again. "Get the fuck out of my house!" he yelled.

I picked up Kalive and wrapped him in a sheet. With a lowered head I said, "Just give me a few minutes to grab the rest of my things." I don't know where I was going to stay but I knew it couldn't be there.

"Not talking about you," he said rotating his head in Wet Faye's direction. "I'm talking about this bitch!"

Wet Faye stood up, her jaw dropped and a tear formed in her good eye. "But, daddy, she was the one who started this! Look at my face!"

"I know, but I can't have you around my nephew. Bernice is trouble, there's no doubt about it but she's also blood, and so is that little boy." He picked up her eye patch and tossed it at her. It slapped against her lips. "I'll find you when it's safe to come back."

Wet Faye placed on her patch and gazed in my direction. I rolled my eyes and watched her walk out. When she was gone I moved closer to the sofa and kicked some stuff off to make a place to sit. "I'm sorry, Grand." I sat down and rocked Kalive who hadn't bothered to cry.

"Don't say you're sorry, Bernice. Just find a place to stay. You're a mother...but I ain't the father and I resent feeling like one." He stomped toward his room where two junked up women awaited him.

I ran back to Jackie.

It was the last place on earth I wanted to go but I needed longer help. If I had any other baby, one less tolerable, it may have been a problem living in her house. But he slept so much that Jackie got a kick out of holding him. She called him her little fat doll.

"He's perfect," she said one day, gazing down at his face. "But he looks nothing like Otis." Her eyes fell on me.

I looked away, trying to hide my deceit. "He's still a baby, Jackie, give him some time."

After that day I saw her always watching me holding him from across the room. She wanted him for herself. It was obvious. I knew then I had to find a place so I saved up a lot of money from a car wash I worked at on the weeknights, when she was home from work and could look after him.

With her help I managed to put away $600, it was some money but I needed enough for two months rent and furniture.

Tired after working one night, I was surprised that Jackie was still up. Normally when I came home around 10:00 at night, she would be in bed with Kalive lying next to her asleep.

Doing my best to stay out of her way, I jumped into the shower and allowed the warm water to caress my body. Work was hard and soon I found myself missing Otis who I hadn't spoken to in months. Jackie said his number was the same but I didn't bother. He knew I was back, why didn't he check on me? One of the reasons I returned was so if he desired he could find me.

I needed to be held, to be caressed by the one man I had fallen for. Instead I got reminded that I was a whore and he had a wife.

There was one man who wouldn't leave me alone.

Rufus called almost every day asking to speak to me and I ignored him every time. There was no way I was rocking the boat in Jackie's house.

After washing up I was just about to get out when Jackie walked inside the bathroom. I hid behind the shower curtain and said, "Oh, I'm sorry, I'm getting out now."

"No need." I heard the toilet lid slam against the tank, followed by a soft thud when she sat down. Seconds later I could hear piss splashing against the water in the bowl.

Not knowing what to do, I remained hidden behind the shower curtain, one hand covering my breasts, the other my pussy.

"You know, I'm happy to have you back, Bernice."

My eyes moved around portions of the curtain. "Thank you, I'm happy to be back." I shrugged. *What did this bitch want?* "If it wasn't for you I don't know where I would've gone. But don't worry, I won't be here long."

"It's no rush and it's no problem. *Really.* I always felt bad about what I did to you that night, when I put you out in the snow. Don't know what got into me."

Me either.

"You were with Otis, ignoring me," she continued. "I guess I felt unappreciated. I mean, do you appreciate me, Berny?

"Of course, and I wish there was some way I could show you." I was talking to her with the curtain still in front of me. Everything about this was awkward.

I could hear her slap at the toilet paper roll causing it to spin. "Damn, we don't have enough tissue."

"It's okay, I'll get some from the kitchen." I reached out of the curtain, grabbed my soft white towel and covered my body. I tucked it tightly so it wouldn't fall down. She was still sitting on the toilet, looking at me and I hated the way it felt.

"Bernice, don't go to the kitchen, why don't you get me clean."

"Get me clean?" I asked. "I don't understand."

She smiled in the same way Wet Faye did before tossing my baby across the room. "Come over here, Bernice." Slowly I stepped out of the shower and stood in front of her. "Get on your knees." She widened her legs. "And get me clean."

I looked up at her, confused at first. Jackie was such a pretty girl and I couldn't understand why she was like this. So mean and nasty. "Jackie, this not me. I'm not that way."

"Are you sure you aren't willing to reconsider? Winter is breaking but you're still homeless. I would hate to see that fine little boy of yours on the street when he doesn't have to be." She widened her legs like a crab. "You're not paying rent, the least you could do is get me clean."

Disgusted, and feeling like I was going to throw up, I lowered my head and licked her clit. At first I was doing it like I hated it, because I did. But I also wanted it to be over so I remembered Otis and how he made me feel.

Placing my hands on her thighs I licked her like I loved it. I could hear her moan louder and paid attention closely. I made sure to hit the same spot in the exact way, hoping she'd cum sooner. Before I knew it I could taste her bitter cream as she exploded on my tongue.

I jumped up, turned the sink on and rinsed my mouth. She didn't smell but being with a woman made my skin crawl. With her taste still on my tongue I decided to brush my teeth.

Hard.

"Come on, it's not that bad now," she giggled.

Silence.

"Well, even if it was you ate me like you loved it." She stood up and flushed the toilet. "And I'm gonna need some of that again, next time without all the back talk."

She walked out and when she was gone I threw up in the toilet.

When I was done I put my clothes on, went into the living room and picked up the phone. Dialing a number I saved to memory I waited for him to answer. "Hey, Otis, it's Bernice. Listen...I...I need to get right tonight."

"Damn, didn't think I would hear from you again. Thought you were mad since I couldn't get you a place to stay."

I did reach out to him when I first came home with the baby. And yes, I was angry when he couldn't help. We lied about the baby being his for so long that I actually started to believe it.

"No, I understood," I lied.

I could sense his relief and for some reason that made me want him even more. Maybe he didn't reach out because he thought I was still angry. Now things made sense.

"I'll grab some brandy and be there in an hour."

"No...this time I need something different." I twirled the white phone cord around my index finger. "Something harder.""

I could hear him smiling. "In that case I'll be there in twenty."

By T. Styles

CHAPTER NINE
PRESENT DAY

The van moved at a much slower pace, indicating they were almost at their final resting place. Timo's weeping irritated Barrie to no end. "You need to man the fuck up," Barrie said through clenched teeth. He couldn't see him but he knew his voice. "Ain't nothing more you can do but die so get ready."

Timo sniffled a little, wiped his nose with the back of his hand and did his best to slow his breaths. "Do you...you think...do you think God gonna...gonna punish us? For everything we did?"

"Who you asking?" Kali said.

"He not asking me," Barrie snapped. "He already knows how I feel about matters of the heart. Whatever I did I stand by and if God don't let me in the pearly gates of heaven, or whatever the fuck, then so be it. Give me my bullet and make it quick."

"We're about to...to...be murdered and you...you don't care." Timo's nervous energy caused Barrie discomfort, because although he couldn't see him through the blindfold, he could sense his fear.

"It's not about caring. I can't take anything back I did."

Kali laughed.

"What's so fucking funny?" Barrie snapped.

"If you could take the things back you did, would you?" Kali paused. "Because that's the real question."

"We not children so I'm not answering that."

"Humor me," Kali said more firmly.

Barrie shifted a little. "I haven't done anything that I don't stand by. I haven't done anything that will keep me up at night. So if I have to die, wearing my sins around my neck then I'm okay with it."

"I wish I could...could be like you," Timo said through chattering teeth. "A...a heartless mothafucka that don't care...care...about anybody."

The van stopped and the air appeared to be sucked out of the vehicle. It was time to die and the tension was thick. "Before we get out I have a plan," Kali whispered to the men.

"You just telling us now?" Barrie asked. "They're about to yank us out of here and you do this now?"

"Better late than dead." He paused. "Now listen, I have a gun stuck under the van."

"This...this...your...your van?"

Kali sighed. "Yeah, when they got me I was at the gas station." He laughed and shook his head. "They let me fill this bitch up and everything, then snatched me before I could get back inside."

"Do you know who they are?" Barrie asked.

He sighed. "I have an idea. If it's true that the two of you robbed a stash house then I'm thinking the three of us angered the same man. If that's the case the men who got us are The Vanishers and they don't negotiate. If we want out of this we have to kill them."

"Oh, no...please...please don't say that," Timo whined and squirmed around.

"I take it by your response that you know that once a month they pick up every man on the list and dispose of them swiftly. Nobody ever knows the date or time."

"So...so...we can't offer them money?" Timo asked. "There's really...really, no way out of this?"

"They want your life," Kali said harshly. "Now listen, we don't have a lot of time. There's a holster I keep under this van with my gun. When they open those doors I need one of you to trip me or shove me out. When you do I'll grab the weapon and free both of you. And so there's no confusion I choose you, Barrie."

"Why didn't you tell us this shit before?" Barrie snapped. "We could've been talked about the details."

"Didn't know if I could trust you," Kali continued.

"And that's changed now?"

"No, the only problem now is that I don't have a choice. If we work together we can get out of this, now are you with me or not?"

Silence.

"Yeah, I'm with it," Barrie said.

"Me too." Timo replied.

"Wait, what about your hands?" Barrie whispered. "Aren't they tied?"

"Got out of them five minutes ago, while you niggas were running your mouths."

Keys jingled and suddenly the back door whisked open, the glow from the moonlight shined upon their sweaty faces.

PART TWO

CHAPTER TEN
1973 - 4 YEARS LATER

I was propped in the corner of the living room...high. My warm saggy titties hung down and drooped outward, next to my inner arms. The heroin needle tinged with my blood plopped out of my vein and pricked my thigh. The black leather belt on my bicep loosened each second because I stopped tugging at it the moment the needle did its job.

I don't know where Otis got this recent bump but it had me feeling in a way not always possible. My entire body felt as if I were lying on a soft beach, right before a warm ocean wave washed over me, taking away my regrets.

With my high in place I was no longer a bad mother or woman.

At this point in my junkie career I would do anything to get high and I often did. Otis may have hit me off every now and again, on his way to get some pussy, but he didn't supply my daily habit. That job belonged exclusively to me. There were moments where I could feel the love I had for him, swelling my heart, making it throb so much I felt pain. And other times I believed he liked what I'd become...a shell of the woman I used to be.

And I hated him.

But I was a heroin addict.

And he was all I had. Besides, there weren't many men in the market for 22-year-old dope fiends with a four-year-old son in tow.

The tingling sensation feels stronger in my stomach before spreading outward, making each part of my body come alive. In ecstasy my head dropped backwards, knocking against the wall. Within seconds I could feel my bladder release, coating everything beneath me in tepid urine. When I tried to get up, my eyes rolled backwards and all I could do was remain where I was.

And then I heard the front door open, followed by her voice.

"I can't believe this shit!" Jackie yelled as I managed to open my eyes and look in her direction. "You sitting on my living room floor doing this shit again! What the fuck is wrong with you? You too grown for this shit!"

When my head dropped forward I could see a glimpse of my son before my gaze fell again. It was as if my head was too heavy to hold straight. "I'm sorry, Jackie." I closed my mouth when a glob of slob fell out and slapped against my lap. "I wasn't feeling good."

"Sorry ain't enough! And you weren't feeling good because you a dope head! I'm the one taking care of you and Kalive. All you do is sit around here and 'get right'. I wish you would just kill yourself and be done with it already. I mean, what are you waiting for?"

I moved my head slowly upward. When I did I saw the sadness in Kalive's face. Even at four years old he never cried, just observed everything closely, like he was trying to learn how to be through me. His body had gotten chubbier over the years but his cute face and new clothing made him attractive.

Although everything seemed foggy, I noticed the shopping bags she held in her hands and the new clothing Kalive wore. As the years went by it was obvious that she was stealing my son and because my habit was too important, all I could do was stand by.

"You right," I said, the effects of the drug wearing off. "I got to do better for my son."

"Bitch, you beyond doing better for Kalive because as far as I'm concerned I'm his mother. As a matter of fact let me address this shit right now." She sat on the edge of the couch and pulled my son's hand toward her. Placing her hands on his shoulders she looked into his eyes. "From here on out I'm your mother."

"But, mommy is there," he said pointing at me.

She pressed his hand down and grabbed his shoulders harder. "That's not your mother, Kalive." Her voice was firm and I saw him tensing up. "She's not even able to take care of herself. I'm your mother because I take care of you. She just lives here...do you understand?"

"Don't do that," I said, my voice slurring. "You're confusing him."

"The only one who's confused around here is you." She stood up and looked at me with hardened disgust. "Get up and clean my fucking floor! Or find some place else to stay." She stomped toward the back of the house and slammed the door.

Immediately after she disappeared Kalive ran to the bathroom and returned with a ball of toilet paper. He handed it to me.

So sweet.

I would cry if I wasn't high. I guess he remembered she said I pissed on myself and wanted me to have the tissue to wipe up. His innocence was pure, untouched, and I wondered would it always remain.

I looked up at him, with blurred vision. Slowly I pulled my lips apart and said, "I'm sorry, Kalive. One day, one day, I'm going to do good by you. Don't give up on me, okay?"

I wasn't sure if he understood, until he wrapped his arms around my neck before kissing me on my cheek.

"Kalive, get in here!" Jackie yelled from the bedroom. "I don't want you nowhere near that trifling bitch! You stand close enough you'll probably catch something!"

Kalive looked at me once more and down at the needle next to his foot. He ran into her bedroom. When he disappeared inside, I knew there was no way I could allow her to poison my son's mind. I may have been a mess but I was still his mother. I was now going to ditch heroin. Done being a sad case, I wanted Kalive to know I could rise up and beat this shit.

After cleaning up the floor I washed the tub and took a long bath. Earlier Jackie said she wanted dinner so I thawed out some steaks, seared them on the stove until they had a nice crust, and tossed them in the oven. Next I washed three large potatoes, salted them and wrapped them in aluminum foil.

When Jackie came out of her room, holding Kalive's hand, I knew she was going somewhere. "I'm about to buy him some ice cream for dessert. I'll be back in twenty minutes so make sure dinner is ready, Dope head."

I rolled my eyes after she left because there was no way I could rush potatoes or steaks along. When she was gone I grabbed the phone and called the one person I could count on no matter how much I fucked up. After the call, an hour later me, Jackie and Kalive were sitting around the table when there was a knock at the front door.

"Who the fuck is that?" she asked staring at me, and then the door.

I shrugged. "Don't know, want me to get it?"

"You ain't doing nothing else, you might as well."

She cut into the steak on her plate and fed it to Kalive. I always knew she was falling in love with my baby, which was the only reason she didn't throw me out despite her many threats. If I was on the streets she couldn't guarantee that I wouldn't get clean and come back for my kid. She preferred to keep me close and humiliate me on a daily basis.

I wasn't even allowed to eat her pussy anymore.

I quickly got up and opened the door and my brother immediately eased into the house, looked at me and shook his head. "You look bad, sis. Are you even eating?"

Silence.

"What you doing here?" Jackie asked.

He looked over my head and walked into the house, toward the table. Moving for Kalive he picked him up. "Whoa, you a thick little dude."

Kalive giggled.

"I know it's been a minute but I'm your Uncle Grand and I came to get you for a few days. You want to leave with me?"

"Hold up, Grand, you didn't tell me you were coming." Jackie's voice was firm and authoritative.

He looked at her for a minute, maybe giving her a chance to hear her own words. She played the mother so long that she thought she had rights. "I don't have to tell you what I do with my blood. I'm here to scoop him and unless you his mother you can't stop me."

She looked at me and I focused on my wiggling toes.

Grand moved toward the door and it looked like Jackie was about to cry. "What about his clothes?" she yelled. "I just bought him all new stuff!"

"Keep it, I'm sure we'll make out alright for the time being." He walked up to me. "I don't see no blood on his face," he whispered, so that only I could hear him.

I told Grand Jackie bit him on the face and I was afraid she'd kill him next. I was willing to do whatever I needed to separate them, even lie.

I shrugged. "I wiped it off."

"Yeah, right. You just be careful. One Eye Wet Faye been asking about you again. At first I wasn't shocked, since your name comes up whenever she has a problem with her vision. But this time was different."

"Why?"

"She ain't living with me, hasn't been in a while. The dude she's with now said she bought a gun. Told him it was especially for you."

Suddenly, the only thing I wanted to do was get high.

Guess I have to wait a little longer to pursue getting clean.

I'm not worried...everything in time.

KALIVE

The air was thick and since the house hadn't been cleaned in months it smelled of sex wrapped in sheets of stale food. The living room carpet was covered with heroin induced sleeping bodies, which appeared more like corpses.

Mayo Kenny, Grand's latest main squeeze, was asleep on the sofa; Kalive nestled under her large naked breasts. Since he'd been with his uncle he'd become son to everyone, each addict doing their best to care for the impressionable child.

Angie, with the missing front tooth, bathed him on Mondays, which was the same day she had to clean up

By T. Styles

herself in order to attend the one hour supervised visit with her own kids. The guilt of having her children removed by child protective services would seep into Grand's house when she'd return. During those few hours she would give Kalive the attention he needed, by playing with him before cleaning him up. It was as if she was trying to tell the court system silently that I am a fit mother. Her plights were always short lived because before long she'd remember he wasn't hers and look for the closest needle.

Then there was Sarah, who preferred vodka to eating. She fed him every night with a cheap meal she'd purchase from the liquor store. His daily food entailed of cheeseburgers, soggy fries and red apples, which she'd save for his breakfast. Sarah, with her drunken personality, was the one who kept Kalive out of trouble. Her senses heightened after three glasses and she would call his name when she couldn't see him, forcing him to stay in her view at all times.

But it was Mayo who loved him, and it was Mayo who Kalive looked forward to seeing everyday.

Kalive stirred a little before placing a hand on each of her breasts to stand on his wobbly legs. As Mayo slept he stared at her closed eyelids, refusing to wake her. Feeling like she was being observed, slowly she pulled her crust filled eyes opened and looked at him. She smiled and rubbed his hair. "What you looking at, fat man?" Her mouth opened and brought with it the sweet stank of rotten eggs.

He smiled and extended his index finger, touching her on the nose like she'd done him so many times. "I'm lookin'...lookin' at you." He giggled.

"Oh you are, are you?" She tickled him under his arms. "Stop it, stop it."

Caught in hysterical laughter, he rolled over, gripping his belly. Finally her mood turned serious. "Look at me." Kalive tried to settle down but was still in play mode so she grabbed his shoulders, forcing him to stare at her. His eyes widened and he was scared, although she now had his undivided attention. "Never love me, never love anyone like me. Women like me are bred to hurt those we care about the most."

Although he was only four years old, something in his expression told her he was wise beyond his age. Having gotten her point across, she smiled again, lightning the mood. "I have to take my medicine, want to play with your toys?"

He nodded and she stood up, lifting him off his feet. Moving past the shifting bodies on the floor, she walked toward the window on the other side of the living room.

By T. Styles

There was a puddle of trash in front of it and she pushed it aside with her size ten-foot until a space existed in the center of the debris, big enough for Kalive to play.

Satisfied, she placed him down and located his toy truck that Sarah put on top of the refrigerator. She handed it to him, "I'm gonna get right and I'll be back."

Kalive watched her walk to the sofa, grab a tin lunchbox tucked in the cushions, which held heroin and other equipment.

With his eyes now on the toy he ran his palm down the wheels and watched them spin. Running the truck around the little patch of floor, only a few seconds passed before boredom arrived and he wanted Mayo back. But when he glanced her way he noticed her head bobbing back and forth rapidly. Puddles of froth oozed out the corners of her mouth and her body vibrated like a guitar string.

And just like that, the toy seemed a waste of time.

Kalive placed the toy down, stood up and stepped over the trash. Normally Mayo would pick him up and carry him over the sleeping bodies but she was in a strange catatonic state, one he couldn't understand.

Remembering that he was a big boy he passed the first body, stepping on her hand in the process. And then onto the next, whose face could not be seen because it was covered by cascading long wild hair. The third body put him in a trance and he stopped to observe her closely. Her eyes were closed but she seemed peaceful and strange, and before long he found the tips of his fingers on her closed lids, followed by her nose. Her temperature was sweaty and tepid.

A strange feeling took over Kalive as he looked around at the piles of sweaty flesh surrounding him. Their long arms, plump thighs and curves had him giddier than any toy car. For a second he wondered if he could play with them instead.

His stomach growled and he blinked a few times remembering Mayo. Standing up he tiptoed between them and moved toward the couch. He crawled up on the sofa and sat on Mayo's lap. For a second he observed her, before touching her plush wet lips. "Mayo, I...I'm hungry."

Silence.

"Mayo, I wanna...I wanna eat," he said a little louder, this time pouting. He took to pushing her breasts to wake her up but nothing worked.

"What are you doing, boy?" Grand asked walking through the front door. He swooped up Kalive's thick body, and placed two fingers against the pulse on Mayo's neck. Leaving it there for a few moments he exhaled deeply and sighed. "Fuck! Not again!"

By T. Styles

Sensing Grand's anxiousness Kalive looked down at Mayo. He didn't know what had his uncle so upset because in his opinion she looked beautiful.

The thing was, she was dead.

CHAPTER ELEVEN

BERNICE

When Grand called to say he was dropping off Kalive because someone died I hung up in his face. I wasn't ready for the kid to come home. Things weren't perfect but they were calmer with him not around because Jackie couldn't throw him in my face.

After hanging up on my brother I couldn't sit down. I kept circling the floor, irritated by my need to be at Otis's beckon call just to get high. Two hours ago he said he'd be here in twenty minutes and it was three hours later.

Still no call.

No show.

When there was a knock at the door I rushed toward it, tripping over my own foot, falling face first to the floor. Quickly I pulled myself up, tripped again and slammed to my knees. From where I landed, I crawled, turned the knob and looked up at Otis. "What took you so long?"

He frowned, helped me up and walked to the sofa. It looked like he was carrying an invisible large

By T. Styles

wooden cross, and his eyes were downward. I can't remember the last time I'd seem him like this but I was too worried about my hit to concern myself.

"I'm here now, Bernice." He flopped to the sofa. "I suggest you leave it alone."

I sat next to him, rubbing my sweaty hands over my kneecaps as he slowly dug into his pocket. He was unhurried and I started to smack his hand and dip my fingers into his pocket to get the dope myself. Finally he pulled out a bag of heroin and turned toward me.

I licked my lips.

"You gonna sit there or get the kit?"

I jumped up, rushed toward my room and pushed clothes and trash around on a hunt for the kit. I was supposed to clean my space earlier but decided to wait until after my recovery. Jackie never believed me but today was my last day on heroin. I was done with this emotional game and I wanted to be better for Kalive and myself.

It took me five minutes to find the kit, stuffed under a pile of dirty clothes in the corner. And the moment I walked back into the living room I sighed.

Jackie was home.

She tossed her purse on the floor and looked at Otis and then me. She was wearing tight white pants and a red top with no bra on and I could tell immediately she had an attitude. "Rufus called today, said he couldn't get through because the phone kept ringing. Why, Bernice?"

I shrugged.

Who gave a fuck?

"Maybe I was busy. And I can't answer the phone remember?" The last thing I was thinking about these days was Rufus. I was over him a long time ago and preferred not to talk to him. Besides, it wasn't like he could be real. We lived the lie of me being his cousin for so long I started to believe it.

"Busy doing what? Fucking with him?" She pointed at Otis. "Why you always in my house instead of being home with your wife anyway?"

Otis sighed. "If you want me to leave then just say it, Jackie. I'm not in the mood for this shit tonight."

"I asked a question." She stood in front of him, fists pinned to her hips. "Because I know she got cancer. And what do you do? Keep time in my house with a fucking junkie. You're a disgrace."

Wow, I didn't know she was sick. Was she dying too?

Otis stood up and moved toward the door. At this point I was so sick my body was in physical pain. My bones ached. I felt this morning's breakfast stirring in my gut and I knew I was about to throw up. Afraid I would stay like this all night I rushed toward him and clasped my hand around his wrists. "Please don't go, Otis, I'm begging you. Don't leave me like this."

Jackie shook her head, the muscles of her temples pulsated as she frowned. She seemed darker and more demented than she had in the past. "All you care about is that shit, you don't even give a fuck about Kalive. Instead of letting me have him, you'd rather keep him away with your whore brother."

She was annoying me and I felt myself wanting to get violent toward her. "I'm going to get better, Jackie, I just need a little more and Otis is here to help me. Please, don't make him leave."

She stepped back on one of her feet and crossed her arms over her chest. Now she looked conniving. "You want it so bad, let me see you do it. Let me see what has you both so crazy you gave up on life."

Otis laughed and then looked down at me. "All I want to do is get high, that's it, anything else ain't for me, Berny. I'm gonna split. I'm sorry, goodbye."

I knew he was about to leave and there was a stronger sourness growing in my stomach. If he left who knows the next time I would catch dope. "Please, Otis, who cares if she watches?" When I saw my pleas were falling on deaf ears I dropped to my knees. "Don't leave me like this, Otis, I'll do anything." I wrapped my arms around his knees and kissed them both.

He looked down at me, maybe trying to figure out how he could benefit since he already owned me.

"Please, Otis." I squeezed his legs just a little tighter.

He exhaled. "Fuck it, I'll entertain this shit."

He helped me up, sat on the sofa and looked over at Jackie. I thought I saw hate but I could be wrong. He opened my heroin kit and went to work. Impatiently I waited as he prepped, cooked and filled the syringe. When he was done he tied the belt around my arm, tapped the crease of my elbow and inserted the needle. When I felt my weak vein pop I could feel life getting better already. His hand shook as he pushed more of the dope through my body and I could sense his anxiousness to get high as his hand trembled.

Oh God...

The feeling.

He removed the needle and I felt a warm sensation take over. I leaned back on the sofa and through the corner of my eyes I saw Otis busy at work preparing his hit. Using the same syringe he cooked his batch and inserted the needle into a vein on his neck.

When his head dropped backwards I smiled. Now we were on the same plane. His tongue hung out and his fingertips crept toward me, until he was holding my hand.

My head was too heavy to lift, to see if Jackie was watching. I was feeling too good to care until five minutes later. She had pulled up a chair from the kitchen and was sitting in front of us, observing.

"I want to see you fuck him," she said.

I wiped the slob that produced on my mouth with the back of my hand. It wasn't enough for her that we humiliated ourselves by allowing her to watch us shoot up. As always she wanted more. "Jackie...I can't...energy...I don't have."

Her eyes were cold and flat. "Do it or find some place else to live."

There goes again, blackmailing me when she couldn't get her way. I turned my head toward Otis, who I could tell was still feeling the effects. "I'm done," he whispered.

"Why? It ain't like you haven't been fucking her anyway," Jackie said.

I sensed the tone of her voice and knew now what was happening. "You want him don't you?" I asked. "You always have."

Her expression was softer and she bit down on the corner of her lip. "You don't know what you talking—"

"Tell her...tell Berny the truth," Otis whispered. "Tell her how I use to come past the house on the days Rufus would disappear." His tone was light, almost hushed but I heard every word. "Tell her how I would fuck you 'til you begged me to leave my wife, Jackie. And then tell her how I never did."

"Shut the fuck up!" Jackie yelled. "You're a liar!"

But I knew he wasn't and I felt like a boulder was resting in the pit of my stomach. They fucked before. I knew Rufus wasn't her one and only.

"And tell her how it was your idea to get her hooked on dope, hoping she would get strung out and leave, since you never wanted her here."

My head turned toward her. My life was ruined behind this dope. I didn't have anything to my name and my son barely knew me. All this because of a game? "Is that true?" I asked through clenched teeth.

Her eyes widened and then she looked to the side. When she looked my way again I could see he was right. "Even if it was true, what difference does it make? You did dope willingly. Nobody forced you."

Otis gripped my hand and I looked at him. My heart was hardened and yet when I stared at him I saw something else. "I'm sorry, Bernice. I never wanted to hurt you this way. If you remember I asked you once about dope and never again. You came to me." He gripped my hand harder and I looked at her again.

"I'm an addict and I know it but look at you, Jackie. You wear your pain all over your face. When Rufus fucks your head up you don't take care of yourself, walking around with a half braided head and

KALI: Raunchy Relived   147

eyes more sunken in than mine. You no better than me, Jackie. Even if you put me out I need you to know that."

Otis gripped my wrist. "Don't say nothing else…if the bitch want's to see us fuck, lets give her a show," he whispered.

My breaths were heavy as I was still trying to get over the betrayal. But there was one thing she said that was true. I was the one who willingly did dope, not Otis.

Nobody forced me.

The decision was all mine.

I looked over at her and smiled. All this time she was trying to make me feel like I was nobody and here it was, she wanted my man. That would explain all the nights she tried to turn me out, hoping I would be into women. And why she would get so angry when Otis would stay into the night, instead of going home.

She wanted him.

She wanted to be me.

While his head continued to hang backwards, I unbuckled his pants, and palmed his dick. A few rubs, tugs and pulls and before long he was rock hard.

Removing my own pants, I hovered over him, before easing slowly onto the tip of his dick. He must've liked it because he moaned loudly before placing his palms on the handlebars of my hips, pushing deeper into me.

We have done this before…fucked after using, but tonight was different. We had a mission and when I gazed down at him there was something else in his eyes. Something I'd never seen before. In that moment, despite all that was revealed.

I always wanted love. After awhile I thought it would only come to me in my dreams. I never imagined that during a dope filled haze, I would experience adoration from a man I truly cared about.

As I continued to fuck him, when I glanced behind me I saw Jackie with her hands stuffed in her tight pants. From where I sat it looked like she was playing with her pussy again.

I knew she was sick but at that time I was positive that she was worse off than me. She ran around here with her head in the air like she was better. She never let a minute go by without telling me how much of a waste of breath I was. But there she was, sitting on a kitchen chair, getting off on two heroin addicts who were in love and fucking…well.

Suddenly Otis pumped into me harder, putting more pressure on my waist. I grinded to meet his thrust and before I knew it I came harder than I had in my life. He came too because I could feel his warm breath on my chin. When it was over, he kissed me softly on the lips, another thing he'd never done.

"Otis, you had your fun. Now get the fuck up and get out my house." Jackie stood over us, arms crossed over her breasts, before stomping into her bedroom.

I guess she came too and was through with us.

Before she disappeared I could see the wet stain on the seat of her pants. I wasn't surprised because she was a squirter.

I focused back on Otis. "You were different tonight," I said.

Silence.

My eyes widened. "Otis, is everything okay?"

He didn't respond and somehow I knew I would never see him again.

By T. Styles

CHAPTER TWELVE

BERNICE

It had been two weeks since I'd seen or heard from Otis and each day my heart ached. He was the one who got me into this miserable lifestyle and he deserved to die with me in it. It didn't help that Grand called every other day to return Kalive and I didn't want him here. Had Jackie been home to take his call he would've been here a long time ago, but I'm not ready.

I don't feel motherly.

When he couldn't get me on the phone he would come over, and luckily for me it was always when she wasn't home. So I would hide inside, and look at my brother pound on the door, through a corner of a window.

My life right now is chaotic, filled with scenes and events that have no place for a baby. The sad part is it's not even like I have to care for him. Jackie asks everyday when is he coming home before telling me how much she misses him. She even apologized for what Otis said about them having sex and wanting me strung out on dope. But I knew it was all an act, and as long as I kept Kalive away from her, I would have the upper hand.

When the phone rung I jumped up because normally I pulled the cord out when she's home so that she won't catch Grand's call. During the day when she's at work I plug it back up just in case Otis reaches out.

He never does.

But today she's in her room napping because she got bad cramps on her period. I just hope she didn't hear that shit.

I walked quickly toward it and snatched the handset. "Hello." I was trying to disguise my voice.

"Stop fucking around, Bernice! I gotta drop off nephew. Shit is getting crazy around here and I may go to jail for some dumb shit. It's time for you to be a mother and take care of your son!"

The gig was up. "I just need a few days, Grand, it ain't like you —"

"You don't have no more fucking days! You not listening! I'll be there in an hour, don't play with me and not be there. Or else I'm gonna fuck you up on the spot."

He hung up and I placed the handset down. If Kalive was coming back today I needed to get high one last time before I put my life on track. So I grabbed the house keys, rushed out the door and went on a hunt for money.

Before long I found myself somewhere on Kennedy Street in Northwest DC. I flagged a few cars to get some attention but it was an hour later and I didn't get one catch. Years ago, before a baby and dope, I couldn't walk a block without a man honking at me. I guess when you fuck around with this shit long enough it attacks your looks.

I'm living proof.

I was about to get dope sick when after almost two hours a white Chevy Nova pulled up in front of me and stopped. I strutted over to the car, lowered my body and wanted to throw up in my mouth when I saw the monster staring back at me. He had to be about four hundred pounds and I wondered how he squeezed himself into the little ass ride.

From where I stood I smelled the faint odor of onions and I could only imagine what the scent was like inside the car. "Hey, cutie," I lied. "Can you give me a ride?"

He took a deep breath and looked like he used all of his energy. He wiped sweat from his forehead with a white washcloth that rested on his shoulder. "I got fifty bucks for a dick suck. You up or not?"

Wow!

Money talk first?

Suddenly he was the most handsome man I'd ever seen as I eased in the car. I put my seatbelt on and the moment the door closed I noticed it was hot, despite the weather being somewhat cool outside. "Can you put the windows down some?"

He obliged but not without an attitude and rolling his eyes, his fat face jiggling. We didn't say a word to each other as he drove a mile up. I held my breath, reserving my words for when I really needed to speak. As we continued to drive I couldn't get over the smell. The odor was a cross between rotten cabbage and boiled eggs.

He pulled toward a run down motel. "We not going inside. I know some people who let me do my thing in the parking lot. We just gotta be quick."

I didn't care. At least I wouldn't have to go inside and spend more time than I wanted. He unbuckled his jeans and presented the hugest, grossest,

By T. Styles

dick I've ever seen in my life. "Get over here and earn your money."

I could feel my stomach swirling but there was no time for vomiting. Holding my breath, I lowered my head and did what needed to be done. His penis tasted salty and gritty and because he was pawning the back of my head the only air I could pull was from my mouth. He was moaning and pumping and my head pushed up and down like I was bobbing for apples. It took ten minutes for him to explode, his creamy cum mixed with pube hairs oozing down my throat.

He liked it so much he gave me sixty dollars instead of fifty.

"I've never had my dick sucked like that." We were driving back to the spot where he picked me up. "When can I see you again?"

When he parked he looked over at me, I guess waiting on my answer. I placed my fingers on the handle and pulled the door open. "In your dreams." I rushed out and slammed the door, almost breaking his window.

"Bitch!" He yelled.

Not even forty minutes later I was sitting in a cool alley, with a needle in my arm catching my high.

Either it was the best dope I had in a long time or I was so anxious anything would have felt good. Slumped in the corner of a building, I stayed until my high was completely gone.

A purple haze covered the sky when I decided to go home. I caught a ride with an eighteen year old. He had eaten some caramel moments before picking me up and used those same sticky fingers to play with my pussy all the way. I knew Grand would be in my shit and I wouldn't be surprised if Kalive was at home with Jackie.

When I made it on my street I was taken aback at the scene. Cop cars and several ambulances blocked the car and so many people stood on the block I thought I was in the wrong neighborhood.

"You can drop me off here." When he stopped I rushed out and ran toward my house. That's when I saw Grand holding my son in his arms.

"Where the fuck were you?" he yelled as he approached. "I thought I told you to stay in the house!"

I looked at my door and noticed paramedics and police running in and out. "What's happening?"

"Do you know I thought I was gonna have to kill somebody for not letting me inside? Thinking you

By T. Styles

were in there?" He frowned. "And here you are, outside, dressed like a skeezer!"

I looked at Kalive, smiled and kissed him on the lips. I felt bad when I remembered where my mouth was earlier. I reached for him and he came to me, although he didn't seem to want to. "What happened...I was...because the.... um?"

"While you were out getting high, probably sucking a nigga's dick for a few coins, some shit went down."

How did he know?

"Well, what happened?" My eyes were wide as I gazed at the door again.

He exhaled and stuffed his hands into his jean pockets. "One Eye Wet Faye came looking for you. Got inside your house and everything."

My heart felt heavier. I felt so shaky I had to hand Kalive back to Grand or else I might have dropped him. "What...I mean...how?"

"The police didn't want to say much to me, but I heard there was no forceful entry. Did you leave the door unlocked?"

I rubbed the sweat off my head because I couldn't be sure. "I don't think so. I mean... did they...did they get Faye?"

"Yeah, took her away five minutes before you got here." He paused. "But Faye killed Jackie. Shot her in the head while she was sleep. You lucked up this time, sis. That bullet had your name on it. Jackie took the heat instead."

CHAPTER THIRTEEN
1975 - TWO YEARS LATER

Kalive never liked to get up for school but today I'm not playing. Last night the teacher called and said he was sleepy in class and I felt embarrassed, knowing the reason. He has a thing with needing to be under me when it was time for bed and usually I allowed him. At first I didn't understand why and then it made sense, he thought he would lose me.

Sitting on the edge of his bed I removed the covers and nudged him softly. "You gotta get up, Kalive, we have to catch the bus."

He rubbed his eyes with his fists, rolled over and stared at the ceiling. His chubby face was moist with sweat. "I don't wanna go to school."

I frowned. "Kalive, you have to, how else you gonna get out of D.C. and better yourself? Huh?"

He sat up and moved closer, resting his head on my arm. "But they make fun of me...and tease me..."

Without asking why I knew the reason. His clothes weren't the best. Although I had been in recovery and hadn't touched heroin in two years, I was scraping to make ends meet. With the welfare checks we barely had enough for food and rent...let alone clothes.

My recovery was difficult and long but it ended up being the best thing that ever happened to me. With Otis being there for his sick wife and Jackie being murdered because of me, I was done with drugs.

I was done with Otis too.

Besides, I didn't have any help. Grand was arrested for being caught with kilos of coke in his home and they were going to take my son, unless I got clean. It was hard. In the earlier days I was sick a lot and resentful, but some how I pulled through.

Until I was clean I took for granted how good it felt to get up and not be sick. I took for granted how it felt to be a mother. I took for granted that I could live a life, free of worry about my next hit. Selling my pussy and sucking dick no matter how nasty the man.

But now having gotten myself together, I knew there was no way I was going back to that lifestyle.

"What are they saying at school, Kalive?"

He exhaled. "That my stuff holey." He looked up at me. "Mommy, why come I can't have new stuff?"

I sighed, my body sinking deeper into his paper-thin mattress. "Because I made some mistakes.

Mistakes I can't take back, although I wish I could. I'm looking for a job and when I get one you'll have everything you want. Okay?"

He nodded, and wiped his tears away with the back of his hand. Kalive was so sensitive and I often worried about him. If he didn't toughen up I was afraid the world would eat him up and throw him away. "Okay, mommy."

"You know what, how about we say no school today." I nudged him. "We'll stay home, eat ice cream and watch cartoons. Would you like that?"

"Yeah," he cheered as he jumped up on the bed. He walked behind me and placed his arms around my neck. To be six years old his grip was firm and I could feel his love.

I liked it when Kalive was this way because sometimes I saw something else, remnants of the man who is really his father. Rufus Miller. Although quiet, I've watched a creepiness fester in him over the years. And when I recognized it, it gave me chills.

One day I was cooking dinner and when I walked into his room he was hiding something behind his back. When I asked him to show me I saw the tip of his finger was cut, blood dripping on his toenails. After examining the situation further I saw a doll on the floor behind him which had been stripped of all its clothing. Crimson blood drops smeared all over its face.

To this day I never found out where the doll came from, or what the blood he smeared on it represented. I was too afraid to find out and I let it go. But I never forgot.

Then there were many times when I would be asleep, only to feel his body crawling over mine before placing his dirty fingers over my nose. It seemed like he was suffocating me, like he was fascinated with death.

I'll be the first to admit that I know nothing about Rufus's background. I never asked about his family or medical history. The same day I discovered I was pregnant he was arrested, and had been there for years.

Who knew what the medical history held?

After eating hot dogs, fries, ice cream and watching TV all day I was about to put Kalive to sleep when there was a knock at the front door. I looked over at him, placing my hand on his thigh. "Go to bed, and I'll tuck you in later." Kalive didn't pout; his eyes gave way to exhaustion hours ago.

By T. Styles

I wondered who was knocking, because outside of Glenda across the hall with the four-pitbull puppies, I didn't talk to anyone.

When I approached the door I felt faint when I looked out of the peephole and saw who was on the other side. It was Otis, my first and only love. Also the man responsible for my addiction.

I looked down at my average blue jeans and yellow t-shirt, tinged with drops of chocolate ice cream. Knowing I didn't have time to clean up I pulled the door open. "Otis, what...I mean...what are you doing here?"

"Can I come in?" His voice was low.

When I heard his tone, his slurred words, I knew I should not have let him in my world. He was still on a drug I had long ago given up. And his presence held with it a darkness I wasn't trying to reenter. As he walked deeper inside I told myself repeatedly that I'm stronger than heroin. That I'm stronger than Otis.

I just hope it's true.

After locking the door I sat next to him on the sofa. When I realized I was too close I scooted backward. "How did you know where I lived?"

"I've always known. Saw you one day walking into the building. I was on the bus." He exhaled. "Later I asked a few people where the pretty girl with the little boy lived and they showed me."

My heart jumped. "Why are you here?"

"My wife. She's dead." His chin dipped toward his chest.

I felt like shit when a smile crept across my face and I wondered what was the purpose. I didn't love him anymore. Right? Back in the day I use to dream for the moment she would be out of the picture. I wanted him to myself, to sleep with him, to hug him and to spend every second wrapped in his arms.

But now I was over him.

Wasn't I?

Loneliness could make a woman forget about the worst days, in exchange for the tiniest loving moments.

"I'm sorry." I placed a hand on his thigh. "I really am. How did she pass?"

"The cancer got her." Tears rolled down his cheeks. "And there were days, Bernice, long days that despite her condition I wanted nothing more than to be with you. Than to come here. But she was good to me, always had been so I stayed by her side." He looked at me and I saw the love he had for me painted in his expression. "I wanted to do right by her, that's the only reason I left the only woman I ever loved." He touched my face.

"Otis, please don't..."

He inched forward, his leg so close to mine he reactivated memories of the sexual things he used to do to my body. "I'm clean now and I can't be who I was before. I have to be here for my son. I'm all he got."

"Just one more hit, Bernice." He removed a heroin bag from his pants.

The moment I saw the cream colored powder my pussy tingled and my mouth watered. I swallowed the lump in my throat. I did everything in my power to stay away from temptation and here he was, bringing it on my doorstep, with a bow on top. "You have to leave, Otis." I stood up and walked toward the door. "You have to leave and you can't ever come back here." I opened it wide, the smell of the hallway filling my apartment.

He stood up and walked toward me, pushing the heroin pack into his pants. "I'm sorry, Bernice, I really am. Just let me stay here for tonight. All I want to do is hold you, and after that I'll leave."

I imagined him lying next to me, smelling the manliness fuming from his body. Feeling his rough hands caress my thighs before his face found it's way between my legs. Soft suckles, careful in their motions but deliberate in their actions. "You have to leave." My voice was firmer now. "I'm not going to say it again."

He placed his hands on the side of my face and looked into my eyes. "I'm proud of you." He kissed me and I melted. "I never told you this, but...but...I love you and I always will." He walked out.

He had been gone for five minutes and I stayed by the door, looking at the wood pattern, trying to see his face appear in the frame. My mind swirling with thoughts of sweet heroin highs when we were together. I realized it wasn't just about the dope. It was the experience of being so high with someone that it felt like both of us left the planet. Swimming around in the solar system. No worries. All love.

Everything about me was different now that I opened the door to find Otis. I started thinking of what life would be like without responsibility. Why should I take care of a child whose father didn't want him in the first place? Rufus may have been in jail but to me he got off easy. He was able to shuck his responsibilities and leave them on me.

I walked toward Kalive's room, my hand gripping the cool doorknob before walking inside. Surprisingly he was up, waiting, looking my way. I dropped to my knees next to his mattress. "I want to tell you something and I want you to listen hard."

He nodded.

"I never wanted to be a bad mother. I never wanted you to be afraid of me and I don't want you to be afraid of me now. It's just that…it's just that I'm not as strong as I thought I was and over the days you may see me change." I swallowed the lump in my throat again. "But I want you to always remember the good times because what you may see me become is not your fault."

It was heavy I know, but somehow I believed Kalive picked up on things most 6 year olds didn't. I just needed him to know what was about to happen even though I had no clue myself.

"I'm sorry, Kalive, I really am. It's just that I'm a woman and I'm not a whole lot without a man."

"But I can be your man," He said softly.

I smiled and eased into his bed. The mattress squeaked as I positioned myself directly behind him. I tried not to cry but the tears flowed anyway. And when he was sound asleep I left the room, picked up the phone and called the number I never forgot, hoping it would reach him still.

"Hello." His voice was low and I could feel his sadness.

"Otis, it's me. Please…please come back, I need to see you again."

"Oh, my God. Thank you, Berny, I'm on my way."

CHAPTER FOURTEEN
BERNICE

There have been a string of robberies in my apartment building and I think Otis is responsible. We used so much dope that sometimes he couldn't make it to his landscaping gigs. Whenever that happened he got the money the best he could. And since he was supplying my habit, I didn't pry.

I learned to not ask questions, and most times I didn't care. But when my friend across the hall's apartment was broken into, and three of her nine newborn pit-bull pups stolen, I felt like Otis' actions were too close to home. I think he chose our building because he knew people's schedules.

I was fixing Kalive breakfast when there was a knock at my door. When I opened it I started to slam it shut when I saw Glenda's face, thinking she was about to ask me if Otis was responsible for the recent break-ins. Her light skin was painted with too much pink blush and her red hair sat on the top of her scalp in a tight bun. "You want puppies?"

When I looked down she had one stuffed under each armpit, a grey one with bluish eyes and a red nose. "What you talking about?"

"They're already trained, Bernice." She looked down at them and they were so still they looked fake. "All you got to do is feed 'em and walk 'em. After awhile people will know you got protection and you won't get hit like we did the other night."

I looked down at the dogs again. I wanted to send her on her way but I felt bad because she was being so nice. "I ain't got no money to give you for them, Glenda." Otis popped into my head and I wondered how far he was with my dope. "I'm on hard times 'round here."

She rolled her eyes. "You got a man, shouldn't he be helping?" As sarcastic as she sounded, maybe she did know Otis was responsible and trying to feel me out.

"He doing what he can, but we barely making it."

"I know, that's why I'm offering them to you as a friend. You live on the ground floor, girl. You need these dogs more than I do." She raised each one to her lips and kissed the tops of their heads. They growled. "Maybe Kalive can walk them and loose some weight."

I frowned. "You saying my kid fat?"

"No…just…I was just…"

"Why are you giving them away?" I asked with an attitude.

"I'm moving. Can't be around this neighborhood no more, Bernice. I don't feel safe. Never have but now things were worse."

That explains why she was trying to unload them.

Maybe I wanted to get her out of my face so that I could count down the minutes for Otis to get home. Or maybe she was getting on my nerves, either way I accepted her offer. She shoved them into my hands, their noses pressed against my titties. And just like that she was gone.

I hadn't sat them down before Kalive came out of his room, hollering and screaming. The dogs frightened him and he slammed his door shut before I could talk to him and tell him it would be okay. When I opened the door, he was on his bed, his head hidden under his blue Superman sheet. Most of his body may have been covered but I could still see the white cast on his arm.

Over the past six months, since I was back on dope, he took his anger out on me in slight ways. He would write the word 'hate' on the wall in red crayon. Or piss on the floor in the bathroom, only for me to wake up in the middle of the night to urine on my toes. He made it clear about how he felt about me. But it was the time he stole my dope in a halfhearted attempt to get me clean that caused us serious problems.

That day Otis left early for work and left me something in my pink toothbrush case like always. I stuffed it under the cushions of the sofa but Kalive must've known about my hiding place because when I woke up to take my morning hit it was gone. I spent two hours tearing the place apart when Otis finally called. "Calm down, woman. I can barely make out what you saying."

With wild eyes staring around the apartment as I held the handset to my ear I accused him of everything under the sun. "You took my hit, you black mothafucka! You took my hit knowing I would be sick! You want me to die, don't you? Just say it!"

"Why would I do that? Huh? Give me one reason why I would take something I gave to you? I love you, Berny."

"If it wasn't you than who was it?"

At that time Kalive walked out of his room, guilt spread over his face like a second skin. I knew this look well because he would steal money from Otis to buy snacks at school, wearing the same expression on his face. He knew exactly where my dope was I was certain.

With the revelation I quickly hung up on Otis and stormed in his direction. Looking down at him I held out my hand. "Give it to me, Kalive. Give it to me or I'm going to get very angry." I could feel cool air rushing up my widened nostrils, before turning hot when I breathed out.

"I don't have —"

I slapped him so hard his lip cracked. But unless he gave me my dope I had no intentions of stopping. "I said…give…it…to…me."

I extended my hand and waited for him to pull my dope from wherever he'd hidden it. Instead he took two quick breaths and looked dead into my eyes. "I…don't…have…it."

I found it hard to understand Kalive at times. He was afraid of everyone else in the world, but me. He would act out, curse at me and even tell me he wish I wasn't his mother. I may have been on dope but I didn't do shit to deserve his treatment.

It's hard to say everything that happened after he refused to give me my heroin. Maybe I choose to forget most of the things. In the end I was standing behind him, bending his arm back so far it popped out the socket. He hadn't been a fan in years, but in that moment I am certain I lost him for good.

Could it be possible for a six year old to maintain hate for so long?

In Kalive's case I'd have to say yes.

I walked into his room with the dogs. "They're just puppies, Kalive. Why you scared?"

His body remained hidden. "I don't like them! Get them out!"

I exhaled.

Fuck his punk ass!

"Well you gonna have to get over it because they live here now. Unless you gonna stay in this room forever." I slammed his bedroom door and stormed into the living room.

I sat them on the floor and thought about my man. As I watched the puppies play I thought about Otis and Kalive's relationship, which had blossomed.

Otis had been using heroin longer than me, so he had more moments of clarity than I did. I think during those times he would talk to Kalive, man to man and Kalive adored those moments. Otis always said he regretted never having children and he would not waste the opportunity to do the best he could for Kalive, even if he was always high.

In return Kalive worshipped him, often giving him the love I thought should've been reserved for me. Maybe I'm sick for having these thoughts. To weak to pull myself out of the habit but angry that there always seems to be someone waiting to pick up where I left off as his parent.

When there was another knock at the door I rushed toward it. It was a little too early for Otis to be home but maybe I was wrong. He would do that from time to time when he wanted a high or missed me. The only thing is he has a key.

I pulled the door open, with a smile on my face. But who I saw caused my bowels to loosen.

Standing in front of me was Rufus. I hadn't seen him in almost seven years.

I stumbled backwards. The air seemed to thicken making it hard to breathe.

"Aren't you happy to see me?" He smiled, his teeth whiter than baby powder. "Because I'm happy to see you."

My feet felt planted. As my eyes glanced over his body I saw muscular arms and a chiseled physique, like he'd been working out and taking care of himself...*well*. Even his skin was smooth and unconsciously I rubbed my hand over my cratered face, due to years of running down the street looking for money to buy dope, many times when the sun was at it's highest.

"Why you touching your cheek?" He laughed, pushing my hand down. He was always so aggressive and I remembered that was one of the things that frightened me. "You still as beautiful as I remember."

Lies. Lies.

I spread my pasty lips apart. "What...what are you doing here?"

His stance stiffened, as if I just disrespected his mother, calling her out of her name. "I came back for you and my family. Didn't Otis tell you?"

More rumble in my gut and this time it felt like I wouldn't be able to stop myself from defecating in my pants. "No, he…he never mentioned a word."

"That's funny, I told him to keep in touch with you over the years. After Jackie was murdered I knew you would need company but I guess he didn't do that right." He paused. "And if you're worried if I blame you for what happened to her I don't. This is life and shit be that way at times."

Shit be that way at times? Shouldn't he care I was responsible? That she died because Faye was looking for me?

It was clear that he never really cared about her, so why would I think he would care about me?

Did he know that Otis and I were a couple, or was he just baiting me like always, trying to get me to tell on myself?

So many questions.

So little time!

"Have you seen him? Otis?" His brows lowered. "Because I haven't been able to find that fool in almost a year. After he gave me this address and said he saw you. It was right before his wife died."

He looked at me intensely and I rushed toward the bathroom without responding. I sat on the toilet for thirty minutes, hoping that when I returned he'd be gone and that this would all be a dream. I wanted him to go on with his life and leave me with his best friend and my only confidant.

Realizing I could hide no more, I took two deep breaths, opened the door and walked toward the living room. Rufus was still there, sitting on the sofa. Only now Kalive was next to him, his knees buried in his chest because the puppies played around on the floor in front of him. Rufus was whispering something to him and I wondered was it about me, or Otis.

It had only been an hour since those dogs were here and already they took a shit in the threshold of the hallway. I walked over the pile and moved nervously toward Rufus and Kalive.

"I see you been feeding him but why didn't you tell him about his father?" Rufus stared up at me while talking down to me like I was a child. "He said he didn't know I existed. What kind of woman would not tell a boy about his daddy?"

I looked at Kalive and he blinked rapidly.

"Rufus, you haven't been in his life. *Ever*. Didn't even want me to have him remember? Why would I tell him about you?"

He frowned and then smiled.

He's so creepy.

"Shit, woman, I was just jiving you. What I look like having something as fine as you kill my seed? Huh? Of course I wanted you to have my son. I gave him to you didn't I?" He glanced at Kalive again as if just seeing him for the first time. "He's perfect. Looks just like me. He probably acts like me too, doesn't he?"

Silence.

Rufus rubbed his hair roughly and Kalive backed away. I don't think he wanted to be touched and Rufus seemed not to notice his stiff posture but I did. "What happened to his arm?"

"It broke."

"You gotta be more careful. A child is a woman's responsibility. Not everyone can live up to the call." He looked at Kalive again. "What's your name?"

"Kalive. Kalive Davenport."

Rufus shot me a look I felt in the center of my gut. "My last name's Miller. Why isn't his?"

"I'll change it next week." I smiled, my teeth chattering. "Kalive Miller it is."

Why doesn't he leave us alone? Go back to jail! Please!

When the front door opened I started to run to the bathroom again when Otis walked inside. Holding a brown bag, at first he didn't seem to notice Rufus. Kalive did, and he rushed up to him no longer caring about the pups that were now nipping at each other in the kitchen. Excited he wrapped his arms around Otis' leg.

Otis greeted him with love, still clueless that we had company. When he finally noticed he looked as sick as I did earlier. "Rufus...you home."

Rufus stood up and walked toward him, hands stuffed in his blue jean pockets. "Go in the room, son," Rufus told Kalive. When he didn't budge he plucked him in the head so hard I flinched. "I said go to your room."

Kalive placed his hand and his cast on top of his head and ran into his room crying, the door slamming behind him.

"What are you doing here, Otis? Why you using keys to enter my woman's place?"

Otis seemed confused, tossed up even and I thought he would lose his guts even though we both knew it was bound to happen. We talked about it last week, the day when he would get out. And there he was.

"I was seeing about her, Rufus, that's all, blood." Otis placed the paper bag on the floor and put a firm hand on Rufus' shoulder. Rufus stared at it so hard Otis snatched it away as if it were on fire. "I'm just making sure the world didn't get her and the boy. You know...like I promised."

"So basically you fucking my bitch?"

I placed an opened hand on my belly, deciding to get into the conversation. "Rufus, we haven't been together in —"

"Shut the fuck up, Bernice, I'm talking to a man who's old enough to speak for himself." Rufus stared at me and then focused on Otis. "So you been fucking her for how long?"

I don't think Otis liked how he spoke to me. His stance was more upright and I saw a glimmer in his eyes. "Let's just say I been fucking her long enough," Otis responded.

Oh no! What was he doing? Rufus moved closer, so close if Otis wanted to step forward he would have to knock him over or go around him. "What did you just say?"

"I'm saying that I stayed because I had to, because I wanted to." He stepped closer to Rufus. "If that was wrong then that's the cross I have to bear but I'm not about to apologize. I care about Bernice, and that boy. That's all you need to know." He cleared his throat.

Rufus looked back at me and then at Otis again. "I knew you been fucking her." He laughed. "Just wondered when you were gonna tell me that's all." He slapped him on the shoulder so hard Otis's legs buckled. "But I'm home now." Rufus's tone was serious. "That means back the fuck off."

CHAPTER FIFTEEN

BERNICE

The other day Rufus came home with what he said was a gift. Clutched in his palm were two large paper bags, inside two plastic ones. Happy that he thought of me after two months of living in my apartment I rushed to him, only to find them filled with cleaning products...bleach, Pine-Sol and dishwashing liquid.

The message was clear.

I spent three days getting the house clean, scrubbing walls, floors, toilets and sinks. Rufus seemed to have developed an obsession with cleanliness while locked up and some days my fingers were raw they were in so much bleach. While I scrubbed I thought about Otis and not being able to hold him at night. Rufus marked his territory quickly, and kept me in what I can only describe as an emotional prison that felt like hell.

Rufus must've realized how much I hated him, because he kept me doped up almost every night. I noticed that his usage wasn't like it had been in the past. He rarely shot up, just on the weekends, or when he was home from whatever he did in the streets at night to earn money. I don't think he would be here if Otis had not been in the picture.

He didn't want us to be together.

I just finished cleaning when Kalive stepped out of his room. "Where them dogs?"

I sighed. After all of this time he was still scared of them. "You gonna have to get over that shit, Kalive. They just animals." I picked them up and placed them in the bathroom. They were a pain in my ass too but two days after I got them Rufus grew attached. They were the only things happy to see him when he came home. When I told him Kalive was scared he said, "A boy can't hold his own in the world unless he can control the inferior species."

So they'd been here ever since.

With the pits up Kalive stepped up to me. "Ma, you got any money?" "Do I look like I got money?" I flopped on the sofa and rubbed my arms as I waited for Rufus. "Now get out my face, you bothering me."

"You never got no money." He pouted. "Rufus either! That's why I hate being here. When daddy was home he —"

I leaped up and smacked him before yanking his shirt by the collar. "Rufus is your daddy, nigger! Didn't I tell you that? If he hear you talking crazy he liable to knock the nose off your face. And then go to work on me. Otis is a good man but he's not your dad. Remember that unless you want to die."

"Get off me," he said pushing my hand, although it didn't budge.

I maintained the hold because I knew some day I wouldn't have this power over him. He was slipping from my grasp by the day and we started to hate each other. "Don't tell me to get off you, I'm your—"

When I heard a hacking sound outside of the window I released him and we both ran toward the window in his bedroom. We lived on the bottom floor and because the landscapers never maintained the grounds, long brush taller than a seven year old covered the windows. The only time a path was made was when Otis came over.

Over the months since Rufus put him out we would sneak around. And because Rufus didn't pay the phone bill and it got cut off, I never knew when Otis would come unless I heard the thwack of his hatchet.

Every now and again Rufus would invite Otis over for dinner or dope, but I think he was trying to feel us out. He probably wondered if the threats he dealt us to stay away from each other worked.

They didn't.

When I saw the wild green brush swing from left to right outside, I raised the window in Kalive's bedroom. It took a few minutes but before long Otis came into view. Once he was there he smiled at us and tossed the hatchet on the floor and slinked inside. "Damn I miss ya'll." He scooped Kalive up first before sitting him down and then kissing me.

Kalive always got first dibs on his love...as usual.

"He here?" Otis asked looking at the door.

Since Rufus didn't have a car Otis never knew if he was home. He was taking a chance each time and that's why I loved him even more. "Nope, he went out to make some money." I kissed him again. "But you gotta be careful, Otis. He gonna catch you one day."

"That's what I'm here to talk to you about." He dug in his right pocket and handed Kalive two Hershey candy bars. "Go, eat that in the living room and be on the look out." He rubbed his hair and Kalive, eyes wide with love obeyed.

It took a threat, a slap and punch to get him to do half of what I said around here.

Humph.

The moment the door closed Otis pulled me in his arms again and dropped to his knees. Yanking my pants down he went to work, eating me out. It didn't matter if I was freshly bathed or if I just shit on myself, whenever I saw him he licked the kitty.

Every time.

After licking me clean he fucked me from the back, as both of us watched the door. My senses were so heightened I could probably hear Rufus in the hallway of the building before he came inside. Kalive was usually good about letting us know before Rufus caught us, but the candy and the television could have him slipping.

After Otis came inside of me I pulled my underwear and my pants up and we did a bump of heroin. It was like we were kids, hiding from my over protective father.

Except this fool was my boyfriend.

Sitting against the wall, the window over our head, I leaned on him and he put his arm around my neck. We fell into the euphoria of the heroin as time passed by. The room was deadly silent until he kissed me on the cheek. "I love you, Bernice."

"I know...I can feel it."

"I'm telling you again so you can understand what I have to do."

I looked into his eyes, trying to get a clue of what was next. The last thing I wanted him to do was leave me. We talked about getting a place of our own, but Otis was too unreliable with his job to take care of me. "What you saying, Otis? Because you're scaring me."

He ran his calloused index finger alongside my cheekbone. "I don't mean to but that mothafucka will never let us be together, Bernice. The only way we have a chance — you, Kalive, and me is if I kill him. Now I know he's his father but—"

"Do it," I said holding his hand, squeezing it so hard one of his knuckles cracked. I positioned my body so that I was in front of him. "Kill that mothafucka." He seemed afraid, maybe I was a bit too anxious to hear the news.

He cleared his throat, reached forward and rubbed the sides of my arms. "I don't have all of the details right now but it's going down in the next few days. How do you think Kalive will handle it?" He stopped stroking me.

I didn't care how he would handle it and if I said that I would've seemed mean. It was no secret that I resented having to take care of Kalive these days. "He'll be fine, you know that boy loves you more than him." I looked down at the floor. "Maybe even more than me."

He grabbed my cool fingers, his thumbs stroking the top of my hands. "That's not true."

"Stop fucking around, Otis." I stood up and walked toward Kalive's bed, taking a seat on the edge of the thin mattress. "He hates me."

He got up and stood in front of me. "Maybe it's because we haven't been the best to him, can you understand that? Maybe after I do what needs be done we can get clean, and start a new life. One that will benefit our son."

I looked up at him. *"Our son?"*

"Outside of you, there is nobody else alive I love more than him."

"I know, Otis."

"Mommy, the TV not working!" Kalive yelled from the living room. That was code for Rufus was home.

My eyes blinked rapidly and we both ran toward the window. Before crawling out Otis pulled me into his arms. "Soon, we will have a better life, Bernice. I love you so fucking much. Never forget it." He grabbed his hatchet, and slipped out of the window just as the bedroom door was opening.

Rufus stood by the doorway, his eyes cold. "Why you in here? And why the window open?"

"I...I was...just getting some air. The TV blocks the windows in our room and in the living room." I played with my fingers, hoping if he looked out of the window Otis would be out of sight, hidden by the brush.

"Kalive, get in here!" Rufus yelled. A few seconds later he stood at his side, lips dark with chocolate. "Was anybody in this house?"

"No, sir, just me and mommy," he lied with a face I would believe if I didn't know my own son.

Rufus walked up to me grabbed the back of my hair and yanked backwards. My neck was exposed and

I thought it would crack. With a closed fist he slammed it down on my nose, splattering blood everywhere. "Kalive, I'm gonna ask you again, was anybody in my house? Tell me the truth or I'm going to keep hitting her."

"No, sir," he repeated, although this time I saw slight pleasure in the back of Kalive's eyes. He was enjoying this I was certain.

Rufus hit me ten times and when he was done, he released me and I crashed to the floor. I was left alone in the room, soaking in my own blood. Three times I begged him to call 911 and he ignored each plea.

An hour later I heard Kalive laughing with Rufus in the living room. I guess they were chums now that Rufus beat the big bad mother's ass.

I wonder if Otis's plan to kill that nigger had room for one more body— his son.

CHAPTER SIXTEEN

BERNICE

He was still alive, one month later…

I was starting to hate Otis for getting my hopes up high although I knew murder took time. I even asked him when it was going down one night. He told me the best way to get away with a crime was to never talk about it and I knew he was right.

So we didn't speak of the plan anymore. Even though I secretly felt he was soft since the plan seemed to be put on pause after Rufus started inviting him over to get high more. Seeing me a few nights a week may have been enough to keep Otis cool but I needed his private attention. I didn't want to share him with Rufus.

Even at the moment the three of us sat on the sofa, me on the far left, as we all took a trip down from our recent high. Rufus made sure I wasn't sitting next to his so-called best friend when I would give anything just to feel his warm thigh against mine.

When the dogs started scratching at the bathroom door I sighed.

"Why you keep closing them dogs in the bathroom?" Rufus asked, rolling his head toward me. His white t-shirt was stained with drool from our recent dope fest. "They animals, Bernice. And animals need a place to roam."

I opened my eyes and looked over at him. "Kalive's scared of them." I closed my eyes again. "You know that."

He frowned. "That's because you making him think it's okay to be a punk. I told you ain't no use in him being afraid of something he's taller than."

My high wasn't fully over and already he was ruining it.

"Rufus, I'll talk to him," Otis interjected. "He probably just—"

"What I tell you 'bout dipping into family business?" Rufus roared.

I adjusted in my seat and my stomach bubbled.

"Because you fucked my woman you think that gives you say so in what goes on around here? With my kid?" Rufus continued. "What I have to do to convince you, that when it comes to my home you don't get a fucking opinion?"

Oh no. Here we go again.

"You know what, you're right," Otis said raising his hands before slamming them against his thighs. "Do whatever you want, he's your son."

"You mothafuckin' right." He paused. "As a matter of fact, Kalive get out here!"

Kalive opened his bedroom door and stuck his head out. "The dogs in the bathroom?"

"It don't matter, little nigga!" Rufus yelled. "Bring your fat ass out here!"

Kalive stuck his upper body out the door first and looked around. When he didn't see any sight of the dogs he shuffled over to Otis first, who sat up to hug him. I saw Rufus' complexion redden. The jealousy he probably felt about Kalive giving another man attention drove him mad.

Rufus yanked Kalive by his arm, forcing him in front of him. "I called you, not him!"

"Come on, man, you don't have to do that shit," Otis said softly. "If you talk to him nicely he'll come."

Rufus stood up and moved in front of Otis. He clenched his fists as he stared down at him. "You know what, get the fuck out my house, Otis."

Otis rose to his feet. "Come on, blood. We been friends since we were kids. Don't do this shit."

"You right, but what did you do? Fuck both my bitches. First Jackie and now Bernice." Rufus's nostrils flared. "Now I said get the fuck out, unless you want me to do the heavy lifting myself."

Otis looked at Kalive and me and shuffled slowly toward the door. When he turned around once more before leaving he gave me a firm look. I knew what he was trying to convey without words. The hit on Rufus would go down in a few days.

And I was glad.

When he was gone Rufus walked up to Kalive and looked down at him. "What I tell you about hugging niggas? Didn't I say that type shit for pussies?"

Kalive nodded.

Rufus took a stride to the bathroom and opened the door, allowing the Pitbulls that I was certain were mixed with monster to rush out. Only a few months old their bodies were large and extremely muscular, with heads two times the size of bowling balls. I was use to dealing with the dogs but for Kalive who avoided them at all cost, I could understand why he was horrified. The animals were intimidating. And for the first time in a long time I felt bad for Kalive.

The dogs with their wide mouths that looked like black holes jumped up on Rufus who patted each of their massive heads. When the beasts were done with him they galloped toward me and licked my feet with their wet rough tongues.

Rufus, showcasing his manpower, grabbed them by the red and blue studded collars around the neck. They were calm under his control, one pit on the left, the other on his right.

Kalive shivered.

"Touch them," Rufus said to Kalive.

"Rufus, please," I said in a low voice. "Don't do this."

He rolled his eyes at me like a bitch. "I said touch them you fat nigga!" he roared at Kalive.

Kalive reached his hand out and Knocks, the red pit, opened his mouth and tried to snap at his fingertips. Amanda must've felt her brother's excitement because she tried to get at Kalive too, only simmering down when Rufus yelled 'sit'.

With both dogs under control again Rufus's head fell backwards as he laughed boisterously.

I looked at Kalive and witnessed a dark stain starting at his crouch, which moved downward toward his inner thighs.

He wet himself.

When there was a knock I jumped up, hoping to get a distraction for Kalive. I opened the door without looking out the peephole and saw Kalive's friends.

They were Jace, who looked more like a young pimp than a child. He had wavy hair that shined like patent leather shoes. Extremely cute, he wore grey slacks, a black shirt and a gold chain around his neck. I knew when I saw him that the others fell in line when he gave the word. His stance screamed boss.

Paco on the other hand was extremely short, and his light skin was riddled with acne. He seemed innocent but the menacing look in his eyes told me he would grow up to be a killer.

The third was Kreshon. He was extremely tall and lanky. His height hovered over the others but that didn't mean he was the strongest. I don't know what Kalive told him, but I could tell by his snarl and frown whenever he saw me on the block that he wasn't a fan.

When Rufus saw Kalive's friends he released the dogs and approached the door, covering his hand over mine, which held the knob. I yanked my hand from under his and stood behind him. "Hey, little men." His smile was wide and he seemed more like a moron than the monster he showed to his family on a daily basis. He made a fist with his hand and each boy gave him a pound.

"How you doing, sir?" Jace asked coolly, his hands clutched at his chest like a grown man. "Can Kalive come out?"

"Of course," he nodded. "He needs to be around young men of your caliber, maybe you can put some toughness into his heart."

"Rufus," I said.

He shot me a look that silenced me instantly.

"Kalive, come on out. Your friends are here."

Kalive looked down at his wet pants. "Can I change my clothes first?"

"No...you pissed in them...you wear them."

Paco laughed and Jace stared at him so hard Paco turned around and bopped out of the building.

Just like I thought, the kid was in charge.

Kalive approached the door and entered the hallway next to his friends. He was beyond embarrassed.

Jace eyed his pants and I could tell he didn't approve. "Mr. Rufus, my father wanted to know if you like that package today?"

I was shocked. Why would Jace's father involve the boy in the drug business?

Rufus cleared his throat.

I didn't know until that moment that he bought our dope from one of his son's friends. He's an awful human being. "It was good," Rufus cleared his throat again. "Tell him I said thank you." He looked at all of them. "Well have fun."

I know he wanted to get rid of them now.

He smiled and was about to close the door when Jace held his hand out and stopped him. "Sir, we had plans to hang out with some girls up the block," Jace said. "You mind if Kalive be at his best and change his pants?"

Wow. I felt like that kid had been here before. He spoke like and adult, and if I weren't looking at him I would not have known he was a boy.

"Uh, no, sure." Rufus looked at Kalive. "Go put some pants on and hurry up. Your friends are waiting."

I held the dogs by the collars as Kalive walked by. I could tell by the way Rufus gazed at me that he didn't approve. He probably wanted to see Kalive yelling and screaming in front of his friends and I ruined his plans.

As I maintained my hold of the dogs I was shocked at how quickly Rufus allowed a kid to check him. It's amazing how he can treat us like shit but around Jace, his drug dealer's son, he wasn't so powerful.

After five minutes Kalive was dressed and out the door. When the kids left Rufus went straight to the kitchen and downed a cup of E&J. Didn't offer me shit. I watched silently from the couch. He was stewing in anger, probably because he allowed me to see a weakness in how he interacted with a kid.

I could judge by his mood that something was going to happen tonight. And since Kalive was gone his rage would probably be taken out on me.

Five minutes later he grabbed his keys off the counter and walked toward the door. "I'm going to find Otis. I'm not about to let no bitch come in the way of our friendship."

He slammed the door so hard I jumped.

I was fast asleep when I rolled over and noticed Rufus was not in bed. Ordinarily I wouldn't care, but so much happened earlier with Kalive and Otis that I worried he would come into the room drunk, taking his frustrations out on me sexually and mentally.

I eased out of the bed, grabbed my robe off the back of the door and opened it slowly. I saw Rufus sitting on the sofa, looking out into the living room. The lights were off but the moonlight from the opened window radiated against his face. Knocks and Amanda lie at his feet and although they were awake they were serene and that scared me even more. Those dogs barked no matter what.

What did they know that I didn't?

"Go get, Kalive," he whispered, without looking at me.

"Rufus, he's asleep." I stepped out of our room, wrapped my arms around my body and rubbed my elbows. It wasn't chilly in the living room but his attitude was ice cold.

He turned his head toward me unhurriedly and I knew if I relented things would get worse. So I walked into Kalive's room and pushed and shoved him until he was awake. Together we crept deeper into the living room, Kalive stood behind me when he saw the dogs at Rufus's feet.

That's when I saw something that stopped my heart. The lower part of Rufus's white t-shirt was covered in dried blood and he was holding Otis's hatchet, the silver portion was crimson.

Devastated, I immediately knew what happened and dropped to my knees, covering my mouth with my palm. "Rufus, please, please say you didn't." I was crying so hard my temples throbbed and I thought my forehead would bust open.

He was unsympathetic, taking the moment to laugh at my pain. "Your reaction is the reason he had to go."

"Why would you do that? Why? He was your friend!"

"I don't have to tell you why…you know the reason."

"Why did you come back?" I screamed to the top of my lungs, wanting the world to know how I felt. I hated his fucking guts! "Why didn't you leave us alone? We were happy without you and then you come into my life and ruin it! I hate you so fucking much! Do you hear me? I hate you and I will never love you! Just die!"

"And I will never love you either." He stood up and walked toward Kalive. Looking down at him he said, "You wanted him to be your father so much, take this to remember him by." He tossed the bloody hatchet at his feet and walked into our room, slamming the door.

CHAPTER SEVENTEEN

BERNICE

It's cold in this place. And I'm sitting on the sofa wondering who this chubby little boy is who keeps looking at me. Every few minutes he will open and close the door just to stare. Why? Across from me, on the kitchen floor, two dogs fought hard, nipping at each other's ears.

What's going on?

"Mama, I'm hungry," the boy said, only his head peeking out. "Can you make me something to eat?

I blinked a few times and looked at him. "Who are you? And why are you calling me your mother?"

"I'm Kalive. Your son. You just forgot again."

Again?

I looked around trying desperately to piece things together. Where am I? Who am I? Rubbing my temples I tried to recall this place. I need to move. Yeah, I have to move; maybe then things will come to me.

So I stood up and paced the living room floor. The moment I elevated myself I felt as if the room was spinning and that I would be lifted off my feet.

Flopping back on the sofa a flood of thoughts washed over me, the past resurfacing, bringing with it an onset of pain.

I was remembering.

I am Bernice and I'm also a heroin addict.

I glanced to my left and saw the boy I couldn't recognize moments earlier. His wide eyes, dark hair and small mole on his chin. He was my son. I gave birth to him but what else was missing?

"Ma, can I have something to eat?" he asked again causing me more irritation. I needed air and at the same time I felt responsibility for another human.

I blinked a few times. "Uh...yes. You can...you can have something." I pointed at the kitchen.

"Can you cook it for me?"

"Oh, yeah, sure." I stood up and walked toward the kitchen, past the fighting dogs. When I pulled open the refrigerator I was surprised to see it was empty. Except a carton of eggs, some old cheese slices that curled up on the edges forming a dark orange rim.

Suddenly more memories returned causing me to feel unsteady. Four months ago Rufus killed the only man I ever loved and I hated the world around me. I wasn't just an addict; I was a grieving lover.

They found his body within the soft ground of an oak tree that sat in front of an abandoned house. There were no leads on the case and many times I thought about giving the police the answers.

If only I was stronger.

I closed the refrigerator and approached Kalive's bedroom door. "I need to get something, there's…there's nothing in here." I walked to the couch and looked around, my thoughts still fleeting. I turned my head toward him. "Where is my purse?"

Staying behind the door he pointed at another. "There. In your room."

"Thank you." I nodded and smiled. Stumbling toward my bedroom I opened the door. On the bed was a brown leather purse, which looked like it had been rummaged through. Did I do this before? With my bag in hand I walked into the living room, slowly recalling more. Except I didn't want more memories, or blasts from the past.

I wanted relief.

I wanted heroin.

I pushed things aside in the purse looking for money. It was empty. "Where's Rufus?"

"He's been gone for a few days."

I nodded although not sure why. "Did he say when he was coming back?"

He shook his head no.

"I'll go get something to eat and I'll be back." I headed toward the front door, looking back at him once before leaving.

I was sitting on the curb in the city, at least I believe I'm still in Washington DC, when a cop pulled up, parking his car at my feet. Two white police officers eased out, their thumbs tucked into the black leather gun belts on their hips. "Mam, what is your name?" the officer with the black hair asked.

I looked down at my fingers. "Bernice, my name is Bernice." Afterwards I gave them my address. But I think it was my mother's.

"Well, Bernice, can you tell us why you've been sitting in front of this store for two days?" The red head cop asked, while the other talked into the huge hand held walkie-talkie.

My eyes widened. "Two days? No...I...I just got here. I think." I shook my head briskly. "I was coming to buy some food. For...for..."

Who was I buying food for?

"The store owner said you've been hanging around here too long. We haven't had a chance to get here until now. Are you okay?"

I looked down at the ground, trying to recall everything. Every second brought with it a new emotion and I felt like my life was a joke, with everyone being in on the punch line but me. "I'm fine...I just have to get home."

"Are you sure?" The black haired cop asked. "Because you seem shaken up."

I smiled again before breaking into hysterics.

RUFUS

By T. Styles

Rufus pushed the front door open, his face a sheet of sticky sweat. The smell of urine from the dogs that relieved themselves on the carpet was so strong the odor turned to ammonia.

He tore off his ripped shirt and walked over to the animals that were sitting on the kitchen floor, too weak to move since they hadn't eaten. Their normal process of greeting Rufus now reduced to slow wagging of their tales.

"Bernice!" Rufus's voice was dry and he hadn't drunk water all day. He trudged toward their room, opened the door and saw she wasn't there. "Kalive!"

"Yes, daddy." Kalive's voice rung from behind the closed door in his room.

Rufus twisted the knob and was smacked by the smell of human feces. The whole apartment was almost inhabitable, bacteria floating everywhere. "How long your mama been gone?"

Kalive, who was sitting on the side of the bed, his legs dangling, looked down at his hands. The tips of some of his fingers were scratched with black crayon, representing the days passed since he saw Bernice's face. "Four days."

Rufus shook his head and his jaw twitched. "And you been in here all this time? Pissing and shitting in your room instead of going to the bathroom?" he paused. "Why?"

"The dogs out there…"

"You still scared of them pits? They just dogs, Kalive, they not gonna kill you."

Silence.

His brows lowered. "You eat?"

"No." Kalive's stomach growled.

"Well how come Bernice ain't take you to Ms. Lucy, or the Chinaman? It ain't like they don't live in the building. Wouldn't have taken her more than a second to walk you downstairs."

"Mama said they tired of feeding me, and letting me stay. Said she was taking advance."

"You mean advantage." Rufus frowned. He dug into his pocket and pulled out 2 blood tinged twenty-dollar bills. He beat a man to a pulp earlier for sitting too closely to him on the bus and relieved him of his cash. "I knew your mother was a worthless bitch. All she doing is proving me right." He sighed. "Get dressed…I'ma take you to go eat."

An hour later Kalive was sitting Indian style on the sofa, eating a cheeseburger from McDonalds. The smell of beef in the air, the Pitbulls suddenly mustered enough energy to move toward the sofa, teeth bearing and eyes glued at Kalive's food as if he'd stolen it from them.

Their gaze was so intense that the bites he took of his cheeseburger were careful because the next nibble was not promised. At any minute the animals looked as if they were going to rip the sandwich from his hand, taking his fingers too.

When the smell of the beef caused the dogs to salivate and grow more aggressive, Kalive tossed his half eaten burger on the floor. In that moment the animals showcased who was in charge and it certainly wasn't Kalive. But it was Amanda who received the laurels after swiping her brother with her paw, causing the corner of his eye to open against her blow, seconds before she gobbled the sandwich in one gulp.

Kalive reserved himself to having his fries when suddenly Rufus who sat next to him slapped him so hard the fries dropped out of his hand and toppled on the carpet. Now it was time for round two of the dogfight and it was obvious by Knock's aggression that this time he would be the victor.

With clenched teeth Rufus asked, "Why did you do that?"

Kalive's bottom lip trembled. "Because you hit me."

"I'm not asking why you dropped the food. I wanna know why you gave it to them in the first place?"

Kalive shrugged, preferring to remain silent instead of admitting his fear of the animals again. Knowing Rufus didn't approve.

"Out there…outside of this apartment, there will always be people who can smell fear. They live for weakness that is exhibited in the eyes. And they will use that fear to take whatever they want if you let them. Dogs are no different."

There was one fry left, tucked under the sofa, that due to the dogs large noses they couldn't reach. Seeing the food Rufus stood up and snapped his finger. "Sit!"

Both dogs that hadn't eaten in two days stopped cold.

Rufus picked up the fry and broke it into two. Giving one to Kalive he ate the other part himself. "Kill or be killed, son. Always remember. Kill or be killed."

Kalive was asleep on the sofa when he woke up abruptly after having nightmares that wolves were eating at his flesh. When he sat up straight, he saw the dogs lying on the kitchen floor, their faces gaunt, their eyes staring in his

By T. Styles

direction. It was obvious that although their energy levels were low, that they would rise tall for food if they could only find a meal.

Horrified that he had fallen asleep in the living room as opposed to his bed, he slowly eased off of the sofa, moving quickly toward his bedroom door. His eyes never left the Pitbulls. He had no idea that Rufus had drugged him with prescription strength cough syrup and left him on the sofa to teach him a lesson.

Not to be afraid of dogs, even those which hadn't been fed in four days.

When he made it to his bedroom door, he turned the knob to the right and then the left but it wouldn't budge. Fearing the dogs would rip him to shreds any minute he tugged harder but nothing worked. When he looked behind himself he saw his vicious pets were now on their paws, tails raised high and stiff into the air.

Thinking quickly he moved toward the front door. Tall enough to open it, he failed again because it also wouldn't budge. Just like with his bedroom Rufus had double locked the door, trapping his only son inside. After checking his parent's room he was disappointed again because it was also locked, refusing him entry.

Where would he hide?

When he turned around the dogs were now approaching slowly and so he hopped on the sofa, as if the dogs weren't able to leap if they desired. Unlike yesterday there was no burger or fries for the animals to devour. Not a problem, the primal urge to survive turned it's head and the Pitbulls suddenly saw no difference between a juicy steak and a human child.

Rufus had abandoned him and he had to fend for himself.

Or so he thought…

When he glanced to his right he saw the hatchet, still stained with Otis's blood, sitting on the sofa. Although too afraid to use it, he picked it up and awaited his fate.

CHAPTER EIGHTEEN
BERNICE

I had been in St. Elizabeth hospital for a few days, or so I thought. When I finally got my barrens, and pieced together the wretched parts of my life I learned it had been much longer. About a week in a half.

Things changed when the police outside of the store picked me up a while back. Something about my mood made them think I wasn't stable and I was hauled off to a mental institute instead of home. They claimed I mumbled something about having 188 children, two of them dogs, but of course I can't remember at thing.

The best thing about not having insurance was that they didn't want to keep me longer than I could pay. After I was able to state my name, the date and the year enough times for them to fill comfortable, they released me to the world.

And today I was going home.

Until I got admitted I didn't realize how badly I was addicted to Otis. Not having him in my life, due to being murdered by a man I hated, caused me to lose my sanity. I lost more of my brain cells than I could manage and the doctors said if I continued to use dope I would soon lose blocks of time.

I told him I was done with drugs but that was a lie. You don't stop a habit you've formed cold after being addicted for years. He said if I didn't stop I would get locked up or die from an overdose. I guess I will have to see.

I wanted dope that moment but first I needed to see about Kalive. I hoped he wasn't in the house alone but I never knew what type of shit Rufus would be on because his moods were fleeting, causing him to disappear for days at a time.

Guess I can't talk much.

I'm not shit either.

During the week they locked me up I realized more than ever the importance of having help. What I wouldn't give for Jackie to have Kalive now, because at least I knew she loved him. And would make sure he was safe. With me as his mother and Rufus as his father I didn't see a good end for him.

After leaving my room, I gathered the last of my things from the Intake Center and was on my way out of the hospital when I heard a man yelling behind me, down the hallway. I recognized his screeching voice but could I be wrong? I turned around and slowly approached the sound. When the voice grew nearer I turned down another hallway until I was standing in front of him.

I was right. It was Rufus.

He was wearing a white straight jacket, with no access to his arms because they were crossed around his body. Secretly it's how I always pictured him.

I walked up on him as he continued to scream at the top of his lungs. He was a raving maniac and the three male nurses tried to restrain him but it was obvious that Rufus was stronger. He seemed inconsolable until he laid eyes on me.

The difference in his moods was like night and day.

The yelling ceased and his frown turned into a smile. I was so shocked by his sudden relaxed mood that I grinned and felt comfortable enough to move closer.

"Mam, you can't walk up to him," The beefier of the three nurses said. His hand was extended, his palm touching my breasts. "You can get hurt."

"Please give me a moment, he's my husband," I lied. I went through so much shit with this man that it didn't dawn on me until that moment that I didn't even wear his ring.

The male nurse dropped his hand, although all three maintained firm grasps on Rufus' arms and shoulders. I touched the side of Rufus' warm face with my cool hand. "Rufus, where is Kalive?" His eyes appeared to twirl around in his head and drool rolled down the corner of his mouth, before dangling on his chin. "Rufus, where is our son?" My voice was a whisper, since I wasn't trying to alert the nurses that neither of us knew where our child was.

"Who?"

"Our son, Rufus. Where is he?"

He smiled wider, this time looking more like a child than a man with many troubles. "Jackie...I love you. Do you still love me?"

My jaw dropped.

He wasn't smiling at me, he thought I was Jackie.

He thought I was his dead wife.

I backed away as two of the nurses rushed him down the hallway, his yelling and screaming starting over again. The third nurse picked up some keys that had fallen and was about to catch up with them when I grabbed him softly by the wrist. "What happened...with Rufus?"

"I can't tell you that, mam, I could lose my job." His attitude was arrogant and I felt the only authority he had was in this hospital, so he played it to the fullest.

"Please...I just need to know. You seem like someone who's in charge around here. Can you help me?"

He crossed his arms over his chest and his huge biceps twitched, which I was sure was on purpose. "He's sick."

"I know, he's suffered from bipolar disorder for some time but today he seems different."

"Bipolar disorder?" he laughed. "I don't know about all that."

I frowned. "What you mean?"

"Let's just say he's a long term resident. Since I can remember he's had to come back some time or another for problems related to schizophrenia. As a matter of fact he was in here for almost seven years before the doctor let him go earlier this year."

Suddenly his brows lowered. "And if you're his wife, you should know that."

I shook my head. "You have it wrong. He was in prison not here."

"Mam, I don't know how much you've been told but that man is sick. And if it's true what I heard you say, when you thought I couldn't hear, about your kid. You're in for a world of trouble. I suggest you get him checked quickly or he'll be as mad as him. That I can promise."

He walked away and I rushed toward the bathroom, feeling like I was about to vomit. Once inside I splashed cool water against my face, placed the palms of my hands on the sink and looked at my reflection in the mirror. One side of my head was braided, the other not.

Did I unconsciously look like Jackie after all?

I did look like her, at her worse, and the resemblance made me weak. My light skin was now dark and ashy. I was stressed and the large bags resting under my eyes looked like they were full of my tears.

My mother always said never say never. Now I realized she was right. I had become all the things I blamed her for. A heroin addict. A mental case. And a bad mother.

Karma took me a long time ago and ate me alive.

I've never seen anything like it. As I stood in the doorway, the landlord behind me, I thought I was watching a scene in a horror movie. Except this was my life. And that was my son.

Had I not lost my keys and the landlord not allowed me in I would be alone. He hated me but I was still grateful for his presence.

As I looked at my child, the odor in the apartment so strong it made my nostril hairs singe, I thought this wasn't real. Kalive's eyes were cold, almost lifeless, except he was sitting up looking my way so I knew he was breathing.

What stunned me was not the death stare he was throwing, but the blood on his lips courtesy of Amanda who was hacked to pieces on the floor. The water was running in the kitchen and Kalive was sitting next to her corpse. Because he had no shirt on I saw fresh wounds on his chest and arms like he'd been bitten.

Like he'd been in a fight and won.

Knocks lie next to Kalive and his bloody snout showed he'd also eaten his share. On the floor, a few feet over was Otis' hatchet that Kalive took everywhere since receiving it from Rufus.

Suddenly I felt light and a black shadow seemed to take over my vision. My legs felt weak and I passed out.

CHAPTER NINETEEN

BERNICE

He'd eaten a dog…

He said he was hungry and since Rufus and I left him in the house for almost two weeks alone he did what he had to do. I was trying to understand how anyone, let alone a child could resort to such behavior but I couldn't. I was heavy emotionally and as I looked over at him as we rode in the cab, on our way to a hotel, I realized months later I was still scared.

I didn't recognize this child.

He was thin, having lost most of his baby fat.

Since the apartment complex successfully evicted us and we had no place to go, I was left to take care of us by myself. We were gonna be able to stay if we caught up on rent and gave up Knocks, which we did. Things were okay until Kalive got to messing with neighborhood pets.

One dog, named Dingo, lived at the Phillips residence and Kalive's antagonizing ways caused the police to keep showing up at the complex. I told the officers he was afraid of animals, even though I knew what he did to Amanda. My lies were useless because no one believed me anyway. They claimed he was choking it, tossing it around the yard and things like that. But it wasn't until the dog went missing that things got heavy.

I guess after killing Amanda he hated dogs and acted out his frustrations on animals that didn't belong to us. There was more to it though. I found out later some little girl named Harmony Phillips lived there that he probably likes. He claimed to be just playing with his friends Paco and Kreshon when he hung around her house but the officers said his eyes showed them something different. I wanted Kalive nowhere near the property. Not only was he not supposed to be messing with dogs but also a known pedophile lived in that house.

When the dog went missing and I asked if he did something to it he rolled his eyes and stormed into his bedroom. Two weeks later the landlord got angry about the increased police presence around the complex and threw us out.

I was realizing that I wasn't qualified to be a parent even though I figured that out a long time ago.

Before going into our room I bought Kalive some McDonald's, and while he ate I made a phone call, staring at him periodically like he was some wild animal about to eat me like he'd done Amanda. The phone rang once before he finally answered. "Grand, it's me."

He sighed. "What now?"

"I need help."

He laughed hysterically. "When have you not needed help?"

I rolled my eyes. "It's for Kalive."

Kalive looked at me, his teeth resting on his sandwich. It took a few seconds before he started chewing and I focused on my meal.

"And what about him, Bernice?" He paused. "Rufus is out of jail right? Why can't he see about his kid?"

I needed him to feel sorry for me because I could tell by the sound of his voice that he was at his end. I just hoped it worked. "He left me, to get off heroin. I don't have nobody else I can go to, Grand, because if I did I would. I'm begging you."

He laughed again and I could feel my patience growing thin. I would hang up if I had other options but I didn't. "Maybe you should do the same. Get clean. Ever thought about that?"

"I am clean, Grand!"

"I'm serious! I haven't heard from you in years. I don't even know how you got my number." One of his whores recognized Kalive on the bus one day and gave it to me. "You didn't send me money when I was in jail, after everything I did for nephew. And now you call me wanting help?"

I swallowed the embarrassment. "Grand, it wasn't like —"

He hung up and my head dropped. He wasn't going to help and I knew it before I called but I dialed his number anyway.

Now I really needed a high and an escape. I could hear the doctor's warning playing on repeat in my mind and still I didn't care. It's the only thing that made me feel like a better person and I was prepared to give up everything for that feeling again.

I sat next to Kalive on the bed and when he looked over at me, brows lowered, I scooted a few feet away. Maybe I should get him help. Maybe he needed a doctor. But what if he told of all of the things that went on in that apartment? The dogs? The heroin? The murder of Otis? I might get locked up and I couldn't risk that.

"Are you okay?" I asked.

He looked at me and looked away.

"Kalive, I'm talking to you." My voice was angry.

"You 'bout to get high again?" he grabbed a few fries out the bag and stuffed them into his mouth.

I slapped him so hard he stopped chewing. Unlike when I struck him in the past he looked at me, smiled and started chewing again. What was I going to do with him? How could I raise a child who made my blood run cold?

"I'm sorry, Kalive." I exhaled.

"No you not." His nostrils flared as he continued to eat.

I stood up and ran my sweaty hands down the front of my jeans. This child wasn't like Rufus, he *was* Rufus, and the fear I felt was no different. "Well hurry up an eat. We got some place to be."

He dug into the bag, grabbed a finger full of fries and continued to chew.

Eyes on me the entire time.

I didn't realize the apartment I lived in was so close here. Maybe I move there unconsciously, just to be near them.

When we got out of the cab we stood in front of the house, looking at it as if it were some shrine, or museum. When I gazed down at Kalive I noticed his dingy white t-shirt was speckled with blood. One of the healed wounds from the unstitched dog bite reopened.

I took a deep breath. "Kalive, I'm doing this because...because I want a life for you."

He stared up at me.

He wasn't buying shit I was selling...I could tell.

"I know you'll probably grow up to hate me...you probably do now. If you do I can't change that. I just want you to know I do love you. I may not have always shown you but it's because I never learned...I didn't know how..." I swallowed, forgetting what I was about to say. "You'll do good here. Things will be better, I know it. You'll see."

He stared out at the house and his silence stabbed at my core.

Why wasn't he saying anything?

Needing relief I stood up straight and let out a quick breath. "Okay, I want you to go knock on the door. Tell them you're their grandson, their *only* grandson and I'll be waiting here in case they don't take you in."

I stooped down and kissed the top of his sour smelling hair. Like a horse in a race he bolted toward the door, never looking back. My heart told me I would see him again and it wouldn't be good.

The moment he reached the front door and knocked, I saw my mother's silhouette and I took off running.

CHAPTER TWENTY

KALI

1980

She pretty. Smells so good every time I see her. She gonna be my girlfriend even though she act like she don't like me. If she keeps fighting I'ma force her. That's only 'cause I know how to treat girls. They be liking when boys be rough with them and she ain't different.

I stood in front of her apartment and looked down at my jeans. I ain't got a lot of clothes but I'ma get some. My friend Jace got money and he said if I stay cool with him he gonna look out. He bought me my tennis shoes and when I was home I hid them in the trashcan behind my house 'cause Grams don't like him. She said something about the son of a drug dealer not being anybody's real friend.

I love Grams but she don't understand young people stuff. She old and only know old stuff.

It looked like my clothes were cool so I knocked once. It took too long for somebody to answer so I knocked a few times more, just a little harder. When I

By T. Styles

heard somebody coming I hid on the side and when she opened the door I yanked her into the hallway.

"Stop, Kalive!" she slapped my hand. "Let my arm go!"

"It's Kali..." I pulled her down a few steps so she couldn't run back in the house and leave me. She did that some times.

"I don't care what it is. If you don't get off of me I'ma tell my parents."

"I'ma let you go but I wanna know why you ran after school? I was calling you after the bell rang and you looked at me and took off."

"Can you please let me go first?" she rolled her eyes and I released her arm. "Good, and I ran because you too rough."

"But boys 'spose to be rough with girls. We the boss of ya'll."

She rolled her eyes. "That ain't what my daddy said. My daddy said boys supposed to be nice if they like you. And supposed to protect you and stuff. Not hurt your arm."

"Well that's what I'm trying to do."

"How you gonna do that when you almost as skinny as me?"

"It don't matter. I can still fight." I paused. "And adults always try to get into kid business. Half the time they don't know what they talking about. I mean, do you think I would hurt you?"

"It don't matter, Kali. Because you not my boyfriend and I can talk to whoever I want."

"But not him." I walked closer and when she moved toward the door I pulled her back again. "Chris be freaking on girls and stuff behind the school. I know 'cause he be around my way telling everybody. I bet your daddy don't know that."

"I don't tell my parents everything. And Chris ain't never do none of that stuff to me."

She was making me mad and I wanted to hit her. I always wanted to hit her but I was afraid if I did she would be more scared of me. Girls are always scared of me and I don't know why. If they do what I say things would be fine.

"So you don't like me?" I asked. She was quiet and I let her go again. "Well you don't have no choice. I like you so that means we go together. And I don't want you around Chris like I said."

"Yo, Kali, come outside here right quick," Paco yelled busting into the building. "Gator out front and he trying to fight you."

I turned around to look at him. "Fight me for what?" I frowned.

"Something 'bout Jace. He out here too waiting so hurry up."

"I'll be out in a sec."

Paco went back out and I looked at Kristen. "I'ma 'bout to go out but when I come back I'ma have some candy for you okay?"

"You don't got no money."

"Not now but I'ma get some." I hopped down the steps. "Just remember what I said, stay away from Chris."

I pushed the door open and rushed outside.

I saw a lot of people in a group and their backs were turned toward me but I couldn't see Gator. When Jace, Paco and Kreshon came my way then I saw Gator. He was in the middle cracking his knuckles.

I rushed toward them and when I passed Jace he touched me on the shoulder. Out of all my friends he's the coolest and I was gonna be just like him. I'ma have a rack of money and everything. The only difference gonna be that Jace close to his father and I don't know mine that good. He in a mental institution. Without my grandparents I would be alone.

"Get him good, Kali," Jace said rubbing his hands together. "I want him on the ground when you done." He looked at Gator. "Now you about to get fucked up."

I nodded and moved toward Gator. My fists were clenched and I was about to hit him when he laughed. Hard. I looked back at my friends and then at Gator because I didn't catch the joke. "Fuck so funny?" I asked.

"Everything." He was laughing so hard now tears were running down his face.

"Well you not gonna be laughing in a second," I promised.

"You dumb, for real. Jace got you fighting his battles and you 'bout to get beat down. For nothing. I don't even have no problem with you but if you get in my face I will."

By T. Styles

I started breathing heavy and looked at my friends again. I don't know why but I was stuck. Maybe Gator was right. Why was I always fighting Jace's battles? Why couldn't he never do it his self?

"What you waiting on?" Jace yelled. "Fuck him up."

"Yeah, Kali, kill this punk," Paco added slamming his fist into his palm.

When I turned back around to Gator all I saw was knuckles moving toward my face. He hit me in the center of my nose so hard I tasted my own blood. It hurt and I put both of my hands on my forehead because the pain moved up.

"What you waiting on, Kali?" Jace said. "You letting him get the best of you? Out here in front of your friends? Damn, Kali, you act like you scared."

The best of me? I can't let nobody get the best of me. If I did everybody would be making fun of me at school.

I didn't care about the pain anymore. I clenched my fists and hit Gator in the stomach and face. I did it so hard at first that my wrist hurt. When I hit him a few more times it started to feel good. My punches got harder and after awhile he was on the ground. I got

KALI: Raunchy Relived   235

down with him and started hitting him more. He tried to cover his face with his hands so I hit him in the stomach.

When he begged me to stop I kept going until I couldn't breathe.

"Damn, he killing him!" Paco said jumping up and down.

"I ain't think he had it in him," Kreshon said.

"I told you, he a killer. He do anything I say," Jace said. "I control this nigga."

When I couldn't fight no more Jace pulled me off of him and I kicked Gator in the side one last time. His blood was everywhere and he was even crying.

"You did good, monster," Jace laughed. "You almost killed the boy."

He dug into his pocket and handed me a ten-dollar bill. I smiled. "Dang, Jace, this all my money?"

"I gave it to you right?" He asked. "You keep that shit up and I can get more dough from my pops." Paco and Kreshon walked up to me. They rubbed my head and slapped me on the shoulder.

"Now let's get something to eat!" Jace said. "Don't worry about it, the food is on me."

When I glanced up at the building I saw Kristen looking down. She opened the window. "You crazy, boy. Can't believe you fought him like that."

"You gonna be my girl now?"

My blood was dropping to the ground and I felt my friends around me, waiting on her answer. If she said no I was gonna be embarrassed.

She smiled wider and said, "Yes. We go together now."

"Damn," Jace and my friends said jumping up on me. "You gotta a girl now! You see what being the man can do?!"

CHAPTER TWENTY-ONE

KALI

"Hello, son, you're just in time," Nurse Radcliff said when I walked in the house. She was packing the bag she brought over that was full of supplies. "Your grandfather's already clean and in bed so you don't have to worry." She looked at me and squinted. "Kalive, what happened to you?" She rushed up to me and squeezed my chin, moving my head from left to right. "Were you fighting? *Again?*"

I walked away and hit it for the kitchen. "Thanks, Mrs. Radcliff but we good now." I opened the freezer and tossed the frozen chicken in the sink like my grandmother asked.

"Well…" She shook her head, grabbed her grey purse off the couch and walked toward the door. "You have to take better care of yourself. You start life out hard and in your old age things will be the same."

I yawned. "I'm good, Mrs. Radcliff. Thanks though."

She shook her head again and walked out the door.

I hated when adults tried to tell me how to live my life. They don't know nothing 'bout what we gotta go through. Don't know nothing 'bout how people treat us at school and stuff like that. If you don't stick up for yourself people will punk you out.

Most times when adults talking I just smile and tell them what they want to hear, just as long as they stay out my way.

I grabbed the Kool-Aid pitcher from the fridge, put some ice in a cup and poured me a big glass. All that fighting and stuff made my throat dry and when Jace took us to Burger King earlier I didn't touch my soda.

I was too busy thinking 'bout my new girl and how she looked when she saw me fighting. She looked like she may have liked it but I could never tell. Girls are weird. The ones I know anyway.

After I finished my juice I washed my cup, put the pitcher back in the fridge and walked to my grandparents room. Granddad was looking at TV and smiled when I came inside. It tripped me out how his face had a lot of wrinkles but his eyes were bright. Like he young or something.

"Hey, son." He reached for me and I shook his hand. "How was school?"

"Fine…" I shrugged. "I ain't have too many problems."

He smiled and leaned in, I guess looking at my face. "Whatever happened it looks like you won."

"I did." I laughed. "And I got a new girl too."

"Son, go on over there to that closet and bring me that bag that's sitting on the floor. I want to give you something." I opened the door and pulled the bag to the side of the bed so he could look down and see it. "Open it up."

I pulled the zipper and saw a bunch of stuff inside. There were army jackets, pants and knives. "Where you get this from, granddad?"

"I was in the military for a while. Not long enough to make a fuss but it was the proudest moment of my life, and I collected a lot of shit. But I also did a lot of things I'm not proud of too. Most young soldiers do."

I sat on the floor, pulled my legs toward my chest and rested my arms on my knees. "Like what?"

He looked at the door. "Like take pussy, even if they didn't want to give it to me," he whispered.

My eyes widened and I fell out laughing. "Granddad, what you know 'bout pussy?" His face got serious and I felt bad for making fun of him. "Sorry, Granddad."

"Don't apologize." He waved me off. "A man should never feel sorry for stating how he feel." He did that funny thing where it looked like he was chewing his gums because he didn't have teeth. "I know you think I'm senile, and I guess most times I am. But I had more problems coming up in my life than I would ever admit to my wife. Those things I remember. One of the main reasons I went to the army was to avoid being prosecuted."

"For...for what?"

"A white girl I dated and fucked a few times decided she wasn't gonna give me no more. Talking about her father didn't want her fucking niggers." He laughed. "I reminded her that she'd been fucking me for weeks so nothing would be different."

"What changed?"

He shook his head. "You twelve years old. Too young to know about what moves a woman but old enough to find out anyway."

I think he lost his thoughts again.

He scratched his head. "Anyway, son, the point I'm trying to make is men in my family have always, always, been violent if they can't get their way."

I scooted closer. "Why?"

"Don't know…think it started with my great grandfather. He was the product of slavery and once killed his white master for raping and killing his wife. Back then women didn't have a choice, especially not negro female slaves." He scratched his head again. "Anyway he made up in his mind that nobody was going to take anything else from him and he lived that way all of his life.

"After murdering his master and killing him, he escaped. He was wanted but would kill any white man who tried to capture him. Before long his reputation grew and some slave hunters were so afraid of him they would cross his path but refuse to confront him. He lived on the run for the rest of his life, took what he wanted no matter man, woman or property." He scratched his head again. "Men in this family are possessive and if you anything like us you ain't no different."

"What lies you telling this boy now?" My grandmother asked walking into the room.

I didn't hear her come home.

I jumped up, kissed her on the cheek and put her purse on the chair in their room. She sat on the edge of the bed and I helped take off her shoes. "Such a sweet boy, don't know what I—" She leaned in and looked at my face. "Kalive, what happened this time?" She touched my cheek.

"Nothing, Grams. Don't worry."

She shook her head. "So old for your age." She touched my shoulder. "Walk me into the kitchen." I helped her up and she washed her hands and salt and peppered the chicken. "I saw your mother today." She flipped a few pieces over and salted the other side.

I think she was putting too much salt on.

"Did you hear me, Kalive? I saw Bernice."

I leaned against the refrigerator. "Where she at?"

She sighed. "I know where she is physically but mentally I have no idea." She shook her head. "My daughter's a prostitute. I knew it was going to happen, heard things 'round the neighborhood but tonight I saw it with my own eyes. I saw her going down the wrong road and I tried to avoid it, which is why I was so hard on her. But my pressure didn't work."

KALI: Raunchy Relived   243

"Grams, why don't you talk to her?"

"Your mother hates me. Always has. I did some things I'm not proud of, reared her up like my mother did me. But she couldn't handle it. Took everything personally. You know...you can shoot a man and paralyze him. And if you try hard enough he'll eventually forgive you. The same doesn't hold true for a mother and a child. Once hate is born into a relationship the only thing that can stop it is death."

I thought about my mother. I remembered her using drugs, dropping me off and not coming to see me.

Grams, was right. I hate her too.

"You hate your mother, don't you?" she asked.

I scratched my head. "Don't think about her really."

"Go see her, son. Let her take a look at you. Let her see how good you're doing, she may feel guilty but if she sees you're well, slimmed out and everything." She pinched my cheek and I smelled the garlic she was putting on the chicken. "Maybe she'll come around. And I can tell her I'm sorry for all of the things I've done...all of the things I didn't do right." She lowered her head and put more salt on the chicken.

Jace and Paco were with me when we walked down the block my Grams told me she last saw my mother. I lied to my friends about the reason for being there. Told them I wanted to get a steak and cheese sub from the carryout on the corner, and since we didn't eat all day they were with it.

Food was never a problem because Jace always paid.

I had my own reasons of wanting to see my mother. I thought about what Grams said all last night. Maybe my mother wanted to reach out but was afraid I would be mean to her, since she never came back like she said and stuff like that.

I wanted to give her a chance.

When we got on the block there were four women wearing little skirts and shiny shirts. Two of them had cigarettes in their hand and one of them was my mother. She looked older but not like she lived on the streets. Not really, anyway.

I thought she was still pretty.

I looked over at Jace and Paco to see if they recognized her. The way they walked toward the carryout without looking her way I figured they didn't. "Ya'll go inside. I'ma fuck with these hoes for a minute," I said smiling.

"Shit, we coming with you then," Paco said.

I wanted to be alone but it was too late. We walked toward them, me toward my mother. When we reached her I smiled.

"Go away, jail bait," the white whore said before pulling on her cigarette. "We don't fuck kids."

Paco grabbed his dick. "Who said we kids?"

"I said it," she replied. "Now get away. You messing up the scene."

We all waved her off and I moved closer to my mom. She stared at me. I could tell she was still on dope. It was in her eyes. Either she got shorter or I got taller because I could see the top of her shiny black hair. Just being near her made me miss her. My grandparents are cool. They do a lot for me but they not my mother.

"Hey, cutie, what you feeling like today?" She asked me. Her breath smelled shitty...like cigarettes.

"What you mean?"

"I mean if you got money you can get whatever you want, I don't care how old you are."

"Leave them kids alone, Burns!" The white whore screamed. "They trouble."

"Aw shut the fuck up, Sandra! Money is money." She looked at us again and I knew she didn't recognize any of us. "So what you little niggas want?"

Jace walked up to me and put his hand on my shoulder. "You want me to pay her to suck your dick, Kali?"

I turned my head and was about to hit him. That was my mother he was talking about, and then I remembered he didn't know. "Naw, I'm good." I stuffed my hands in my pockets.

"Shit...if he don't want a dick suck I'll take it!" Paco yelled.

Jace paid my mother ten dollars and she took Paco in an alley. He was gone for five minutes before he came back with a smile on his face.

I felt sick to my stomach.

"Damn, that bitch was good." He zipped his pants. "Almost sucked the skin off this shit."

"You sure you don't want a suck?" Jace asked me. "You the one wanted to step to the hoes."

He pulled more money out and my mother yanked me by the hand. "He wants it." She snatched the ten-dollar bill from Jace. "We'll be back."

Now I was in the alley and I didn't want to be. She pressed my back against the brick wall and my jeans were at my ankles. That quick. In a few seconds her warm hands were on my dick and I couldn't remember the last time she touched me.

She was about to put my stuff in her mouth when I hit her in the face.

Hard as I could.

She fell backwards and I bent down to hit her some more. I hit her for who she was and for not being my mother. I hit her for being a whore and for hurting the grandparents' feelings. When I was done I kicked her in the stomach, reached in the gold purse on her shoulder and stole her money.

It was mine anyway.

"One day you gonna see me again and I'm gonna hurt you some more." I pulled my clothes up and walked away.

When I reached my friends Jace pointed at my shirt. I didn't know it had blood on it until he said, "Damn, what happened?"

By T. Styles

"I told that bitch that kids were trouble," The white whore said while the others ran to check on my mother.

"You ain't like it?" Jace asked.

"She washed up, I wasn't feeling it." I showed them the cash. "But I got the money though."

They laughed but inside I felt like crying.

CHAPTER TWENTY-TWO
KALI

I'm not fucking with Jace and 'em no more.

After that shit with my mother last week I wasn't in the mood to be around nobody but my grandparents and Kristen. I heard Jace and them were talking behind my back at school, saying I was scared to fuck but I don't care.

It still don't bother me.

After I ran the bath water for my grandfather and helped him inside my Grams came home a few minutes later. Today Gramps wasn't telling me stories about my great-great grandfather or when he was younger. He was talking crazy stuff I didn't understand.

When he was like this my grandmother was sad and I hated her that way.

When Gramps was clean we put him to bed and I helped my grandmother cook dinner. She made spaghetti and meatballs to make me feel better. I don't know why she thinks something's wrong with me. I was worried about her.

By T. Styles

She was stirring the sauce and remembered I wanted to ask her something. "Grams, do you and Gramps still fuck?"

She slapped me.

It was the first time she ever hit me. She tossed the spoon on the counter and sauce splattered everywhere. Her hands were flat on the counter. "I'm sorry, Kalive. I...I just..."

I was confused. "What I do wrong?"

Her eyes got wide. "Kalive...you asked me if I...if I...*fucked* your grandfather." She paused. "You not allowed to talk to me that way. *Ever.*"

I replayed what I said and it felt like I swallowed a basketball. I be with my friends so much that sometimes I forget to change over to adult talk. My teachers at school get mad all the time about that. "I'm sorry for cursing, Grams. I ain't mean it like that."

"I know, son. I know." She picked the spoon up, rinsed it off and stirred the sauce again. "To answer your question, although I don't know why since you a child, no, I haven't been with your grandfather in that way in a long time."

"Why not?" I remembered what he said about taking pussy and figured if she gave him a little maybe he'd get better.

"Things are not as easy as that."

"But why not? I thought sex was for everything." I paused. "When my mother lived with my father she would do all kinds of stuff. I saw her suck his penis a lot in the hallway. I think he liked it there because they did it that way all the time. I saw him stick his ding-a-ling in her butt and —"

"Again with the talk! Kalive, you have to be careful of the conversations you have with people. They gonna start thinking you're crazy. Not everybody's going to be able to take those kinds of questions from a child. You have freedom to talk around here but you must be cautious."

"Sex is wrong?"

"Yes, son."

I thought of my mother who was selling pussy on the Ave. "So why everybody doing it?"

She looked away and I saw her face redden. Maybe I should talk about something else. Grams can't handle this.

"Kalive, did your mother do something to hurt you? Because your mood has been off lately."

I shrugged. "Told you I didn't see her, Grams."

"Maybe you should."

"Naw…I'm good."

I helped her set the table and a little while after that Kristen knocked at the door. She was wearing a pink dress and white shoes and I wanted to ask for a kiss. But if Grams didn't want to talk about fucking I knew she wouldn't like that.

After awhile we started eating and me and Grams put Gramps in his wheelchair so he could sit at the table. Kristen sat next to me and I wrapped my arm around the back of her chair.

Kristen stuck some spaghetti in her mouth and looked over at me. "So where your mama at?" She asked.

My stomach rolled a little. "What you mean? My mama and daddy right here." I looked at my grandmother. "Right, Grams?"

"Kalive, you know that ain't true," she smiled. "I'm your grandmother and there's a difference."

I frowned. "You feed me and take care of me." I pushed the plate away. "My mother's a whore and I ain't calling no whore my mother. So you got to be it."

Her eyes widened. "Kalive, please," she said louder. "You have company."

I looked over at Kristen and grinned. "You right...look at us, Gramps." He was staring at me, smiling. "You got your wife and I got mine."

"You right about that!" My Gramps said, slapping his leg while laughing. He leaned over and tried to kiss my grandmother but she pushed him away. And because he was in the wheelchair he rolled before stopping at the couch.

"Kalive, please stop riling your grandfather up," Grams said. "Today supposed to be peaceful." She stood up and wheeled him back.

"Why, Grams? Kristen don't care if I call her my wife...do you?" I looked at her.

"Not really...but you are kind of embarrassing me." She pushed her plate away too. It was empty though, she ate everything.

"See what you doing?" Gramps said.

I looked over at Kristen again and I felt like my Grams was turning her against me and my head started hurting. "She gonna be my wife and I'm gonna stick my ding-a-ling in her pussy too. I can say anything to her I want."

Grams shot up. "Kalive, go to your room right now!" She pointed toward the back of the house. "I'm sick of you and this mouth tonight."

I pushed the chair back and it made a scratching noise on the floor. I looked at my Grams for a minute and stormed to my room. Instead of sitting down I walked around the floor in a circle.

I hated my mother!

I hated having to live with my grandparents because she didn't want me.

And I hated that my mother didn't know who I was.

I was pounding myself in the head with my fists when Kristen walked into my room. "Kali, are you okay?"

I sat on the edge of the bed. "You still here, I thought she was gonna make you leave?"

"Nope...she told me to come check on you." She sat next to me and held my hand. "What's wrong? I never seen you like this."

"I'm just mad I guess." I looked at her. "I'm glad you came over though."

She let my hand go. "I came because I have to tell you something...I can't be your girlfriend no more."

"You told me we go together, I thought we were cool."

"I can't see you either. Chris said if I break up with him, he's gonna punch me in the stomach...*again*."

I stood up. "Why you ain't tell me he hit you?"

She shrugged. "'Cause you can't do nothing and I only came to let you know what he said." She bent over and kissed me on the cheek, stood up and walked out my bedroom.

I could hear her crying.

I got up too. I got on my knees, dug under my bed and pulled out my hatchet. Most of Otis's dried blood was gone now. And I didn't carry it as much as I use to because it scared people.

Now I think its time.

My grandfather had a strap in the bag of weapons he gave me from the army. Grams took everything except the strap and the bag saying that I didn't need no weapons.

She didn't know about my hatchet though.

I snuck out my grandparent's house and sat across the street from his building all night. I wasn't sleepy and when it turned morning I was waiting for him. Kristen wasn't gonna be my girl again until I got him out the way for good.

After a while it seemed like everybody was getting up and going to their cars. I even saw a few kids from my school walking out the building but still no Chris. I was starting to think I had the wrong address until he finally came outside. He had two boys with him that I saw him with at school but didn't know they names.

I rushed across the street with the hatchet in my hand and knocked Chris to the ground. "Hold up, what the fuck is going on?" He yelled.

My hatchet fell and the back of his head bumped on the step. He was bleeding already and I didn't really touch him. I got myself together and hit him in the face again.

When one of his friends tried to jump in I picked up my weapon and swung at him. I caught him on the leg, his jeans got ripped and I saw blood oozing out. He ran down the street screaming and the other kid followed him.

I dropped the hatchet and hit Chris again as many times as I could. "Leave...Kristen...alone!" I yelled. "Stay away from her!"

I thought he would hit me back but he just balled up and covered his face. He was scared so I picked up my hatchet and pointed the blade at him. "If you mess with her again, I'ma come back and use this on your face. I'm not gonna tell you no more."

"Kalive!" I heard someone yell behind me.

When I turned around I saw my uncle Grand in a red racecar. He came over at least once a week to check on the grandparents but we didn't have a relationship like that. He had somebody in the car with him I didn't know.

"You done?" Grand asked.

I looked down at Chris. "Yeah...I think so."

"You sure?" His voice was deeper.

I nodded.

"Well come over here. I been looking for you."

I stood up and placed my hatchet in the strap on my back. Chris got up and ran away like his friends. He was a punk who could hit on girls but not a boy like me and I felt I should've did more.

When I got into the backseat of the car my uncle pulled off. "This my son, and your cousin Vaughn."

I didn't know he had a kid. When I looked at him I guessed he was about my age but I wasn't for sure. Vaughn looked back at me, nodded, and turned around.

"What was that?" Grand asked.

"Nothing...just some boy who be messing with girls." I looked out the window.

He laughed. "Well you should have finished him."

"I would have but you called me." I looked at him again. "What you doing here anyway?"

"My mother been looking all over for you. Said you left the house in the middle of the night so she sent me to find you. Why you do my mother like that? You know she too old to be kid chasing."

"How you know I was here?"

"Saw some kids your age running up the block and they told me where you were." He paused. "You feel like your business done with the kid?"

I shrugged. "Not really."

"You young but I'ma tell you anyway. Never leave a man bleeding and breathing if the beef ain't over. He'll come back for you. They always do."

CHAPTER TWENTY-THREE

KALI

I told my Grams I wasn't goin' to school. She tried to force me until I said if I went I was gonna get into a fight. Part of the reason I was mad was her fault anyway. She kept asking me to go see my mother and I had to tell her I already did.

"She didn't remember you either?" Grams finally asked.

If Grams knew she wouldn't remember me because she didn't remember her, why would she send me out there?

I couldn't get my mother out of my mind. I laid up thinking about her all night until something else happened. My ding-a-ling got hard. I put my hand on it trying to make it go down but then thoughts of my mother touching it in the alley caused it to grow hard again. So I rubbed it until stuff started coming out the tip.

I think I nutted on myself.

I was so grossed out I got up, walked to the bathroom and threw up. I felt bad for thinking like that because she was my mother even though I didn't really know her. I promised myself to never think like that. But when I went to bed it happened again. And again...until I leaked three times.

My Grams said she was going to make some coffee earlier since she had to be to work. I figured she was moving slow so I ran my grandfather's bath and went into the kitchen to stir some eggs. I took the bacon out the freezer and put it on a plate so all she had to do was cook.

When I was done I knocked on my grandparent's door. When nobody answered I opened it and peeked inside. I was confused when I saw my Grams on her knees next to the bed. Her back was faced me but I saw her saggy skin and big white underwear. I also saw her bra strap.

Why was she crying?

When she turned her head toward me I said, "Sorry, Grams. I ran the bath and put the bacon out...is everything cool?"

"Come in, Kalive, please."

I rushed inside. "Grams, what's wrong?" When I looked at the bed I saw my grandfather was face up and I smelled something I never have before. His eyes

By T. Styles

were open but he looked scared. I moved closer and placed my hand on his arm. He was cold, not like ice but cool.

It didn't take me long.

He was dead.

My Grams stopped washing up.

I always knew where she was in the house because a stinky smell followed her. She stopped leaving the room too.

My Gramps died two weeks ago and she stopped going to work. Everything made her sad and I stayed home from school most days to help. She fought me at first, saying a boy had to learn if he wanted a fighting chance in America. But after awhile she stopped and I hadn't been back since.

My uncle came over with my cousin sometimes but he only stayed long enough to give me some money and leave. He said he couldn't see her like that which I didn't like because she was his mother. Not mine.

My Grams was in bed and I was sitting in the living room on the couch when somebody knocked at the front door. I peeked out the window and saw my friends, Jace and Paco outside.

I opened the door and looked at them. "What's up?"

"I heard about your grandfather," Jace said. "Anything we can do, man?"

I looked at him and then Paco. "No, I'm cool."

"So you not coming back to school no more?" Paco asked.

I shrugged.

"I heard about what you did to Chris too," Jace said. "Don't know if you seen Kristen in awhile but he not fuckin' with her no more." He laughed. "Always knew you were a monster with the hands."

"Thanks, but I gotta go." I slammed the door in their faces and walked back to the sofa.

I was starting to feel madder at everything and everybody. My grandfather told me to check my anger before he died, but I don't think there's a way to do that without hurting somebody. Without making somebody bleed.

And I don't want to hurt my friends.

I just turned the TV on when there was another knock at the door. "Fuck!" When I opened it this time I saw Kristen on the other side holding a brown paper bag. "Can I come inside?"

"I can't have company."

She frowned. "Kali, I know you lying. You do anything you want in that house so let me in."

I sighed. "I don't want to see nobody right now."

She nodded. "I was just coming to say I'm sorry about what happened to your grandfather. He seemed nice. For the time I got to meet him anyway." She raised her arm and handed me the bag. "Some candy and stuff like that."

I took it.

"Thank you for talking to Chris. I don't know what you said but he hasn't bothered me since."

"Jace and them told me already." I heard something moving in the back. It was probably Grams. "I gotta go. I'll see you at school."

I closed the door before she could respond.

When I walked into my grandmother's room she was on the floor crying again. I knew she was gonna be sad for a long time but she was making me uncomfortable. I wanted her to be better so I could have my life back.

This seemed unfair and I wished I didn't care.

I didn't know what else to do so I ran her a bath, helped her up and walked her into the bathroom. I even took some of her clothes off, she got the rest. When she was in the water she looked relaxed. "Too hot, Grams?"

She smiled for the first time in a long time. "It's perfect, thanks, Kalive." She touched the side of my face with her warm hand.

"You gonna be okay? You gonna be better now?"

She nodded. "Don't be scared, it's all a part of life." Tears rolled down her cheeks. "Do me a favor, Kalive." She took a deep breath that seemed to go on forever. "Give me some time alone, son."

I stood up, opened the door and looked back at her. She smiled again and I closed the door and walked to the living room.

I turned the channel a few times and opened the bag Kristen gave me.

I ate everything inside and later that night Grams died too.

CHAPTER TWENTY-FOUR

KALI

1986

I was speeding down the highway listening to L.L. Cool J, trying to make it home to my girl. First I had a few things to do around the way...like pick up money from a few dudes that owed. I wasn't into anything heavy. I acted as a bodyguard for Arab, a mid-level drug dealer in DC. It was easy money since he really didn't need me because most niggas knew not to fuck with him.

Besides, it wasn't like I had major bills. When my grandparents died they left the house in my name. At first I didn't want it, because it reminded me of the grandparents I loved and the mother I hated. I even offered to go down the middle with Grand if I sold it but he said he was good. And didn't want a dime. That made me fuck with him until I found out from Vaughn that he tried to fuck my girl.

I let him breathe because Kristen cried thinking I was going to jail if I killed him and Vaughn got on his knees and begged until they were bloody.

I let shit go but I made it clear that I didn't fuck with him. He a creep nigga anyway. Back in the day he use to get money, but now he sits in that house all day, smokes up all his weed or gives it to the bitches who sit in front of him topless.

I was just about to get off the beltway when an unmarked police car put on its sirens and fell behind me. I looked through the rearview mirror at the blue sedan, which was approaching fast.

I didn't have a gun on me or my hatchet, since I had given up that lifestyle a long time ago. But there was no denying the liquor on my breath if he got too close.

I pulled over on the shoulder and the cop pulled behind me. I may not have had the gun but I had a knife that was tucked on the left side of my car, in the console on the door.

I grabbed it.

The officer, a big black cop who looked like he lifted heavy on the upper body but forgot his legs, approached my car. He was wearing dark shades and no smile. "License and registration please."

I handed it to him. Already had it ready.

By T. Styles

He looked at my documents. "Do you know how fast you were going?"

"Yes, sir, 75 mph."

He took off his glasses. "And you think that's okay when the speed limit is 55?"

"No, sir, I don't. But I had an accident on the construction site at my job and was trying to make it to the hospital to save my leg."

He leaned in and saw my jeans were bloody from where I poked myself with the knife, just enough to bring blood to the surface of my thigh. "What the fuck? Boy, are you crazy?" he yelled. "You should've called an ambulance!"

"I know, sir just figured other people could've used an ambulance more than me. Plus this is man's work and part of the job."

"Well what the fuck happened anyway?"

"The end of a steel beam fell on my leg and almost crushed it but I'm still alive. "

He spoke into his radio and within twenty minutes I was in the hospital, in the ER. Instead of arresting me for being drunk he escorted me without stopping at any lights. The only thing was that my car was left on the side of the road.

After the doctor came in and checked me again, Kristen walked into the room. Since she was nine months pregnant with our first child to me she couldn't be more beautiful. All I wanted was to watch over her and protect her. But sometimes my thoughts grew dark and I thought about doing violent things to people.

Most of the time for no reason.

Every time I imagined death or blood she would kiss me and tell me she loved me. Like she knew what was on my mind.

"Oh, baby, are you okay?" she asked walking up to me as I sat on the edge of the bed, my bandaged leg hanging off the side.

"I'm fine." I looked at the doctor and cleared my throat. "You know how things are on the job."

The doctor was good at ear hustling because he moved closer and said, "You may be fine now but things could've been worse. So it's a good thing you got here when you did. And it's also a good thing that the cop was nice enough to bring you himself."

I nodded. "Can I go now, Doc?"

He frowned, cleared his throat and looked at my chart in his hands. "I'll have the nurse give you the prescription for pain and discharge you right away."

We were in her car laughing...

"Bay, why are you so fucking crazy?" She giggled as she drove down the street. "I can't believe you really got in the back of a car and had a cop drive you to the hospital? Off some craziness."

"It was either that or jail." I leaned back in my seat when I noticed she wasn't laughing anymore and her expression grew serious.

"Vaughn picked up the car for you."

I nodded. "He told me."

She placed her hand on my thigh. "How's your leg?"

"It's fine, I know how to cut."

She sighed. "Today is the day your Grams died. Isn't it?"

I looked over at her. "I'm okay, Kristen. Stop worrying."

She steered the car with one hand while the other rested on her stomach. "Kali, I'm not trying to come down on you. You a good man who's done everything in your power to make me happy, and I love you for it. I never dreamed I would have a life like this. With you."

"It's nowhere near the life I want to give you." I exhaled. "We live in my grandparents house—"

"Rent free," She interrupted. "You so quick to talk about what we don't have instead of listing the blessings first."

"I'm grateful, Kristen. And I know shit could be worse. Just seems like we never have enough money to do the things you want." I paused. "I see how you be looking at Sasha and Harmony. You say you don't want the lifestyle but I don't know if I believe you."

"First of all my cousin is a whore so of course she has money. And you know Jace gonna make sure Harmony is good even though I heard they not together no more. I don't want anything about their lifestyle." She paused. "All I wanted was somebody to love me." She rubbed her belly. "To love us and you're doing that."

"But what if I fuck up? As a father?"

"Kali, you can't fuck up. Since you found out we were pregnant not only did you stop running the streets, or rolling with Jace, you found a way to make a little money, remain safe and come home every night." She exhaled. "But you have to realize that your grandparents dying is not your fault. Let it go. It's like you're afraid to be happy."

I exhaled. "The history of my life...the history with my family, makes me believe that anybody born of this bloodline is doomed. And I don't want that for our child."

"Then change the future, Kali." A tear rolled down her face. "We can't do anything about what happened when you were a child. And I can't act like I know everything you're going through since you refuse to talk about it. All I know is my man, and he loves our baby and me. I would put my life on that." She kissed me.

We pulled up to Mama's Kitchen and walked inside. I placed my arm around her because although she was pregnant niggas loved trying to get at my girl. Her face was cute and her ass was almost as big as her belly. I needed every nigga present to know she was taken.

I had a little limp from the cut to my leg so we decided to sit down and eat. She got the fried chicken and I got fish with fries. We were almost done when some dude at the counter stared a little too hard for my liking. I stood up and approached him. "See something interesting over here?"

He laughed.

I hated when mothafuckas laughed at me.

"Want me to give you something to laugh about?" I asked.

"Kali, please don't do this," Kristen pleaded. "Not again, you promised."

I was about to hit him anyway when Jace and Paco walked inside. The nigga Jace had so many gold chains around his neck and rings on his fingers he couldn't be anything but a dope dealer. I heard his father Rick moved to Los Angeles to handle the drug business there, leaving Jace in charge here. He asked me a few times through people to work for him but I wasn't interested. I was settled now.

It was then that I recognized the dude at the counter, the one I was about to drop, was Tony Wop, Jace's cousin. They walked up to me and we all shook hands.

"Tony, I know you not in here antagonizing Kali," Jace laughed. "You know his legend. He'll kill you and eat you alive."

"Man, had I known it was him I would've thought twice." His words said one thing but he sounded like he was being sarcastic. I could be wrong. "My bad, Kali, I just thought I knew your peoples that's all." He tried to shake my hand but I left him hanging.

Tony Wop cleared his throat.

"So what's up with you?" Jace asked. "I haven't seen you since your grandparents died, God rest their souls." He crossed his chest and looked up in the sky.

"Everything good over this way." I said. Kristen stood up and I put my arm around her. "I'm about to be a father."

They all laughed but stopped short.

"You sure you gonna be good at that?" Jace asked. "Being a father requires a patient man and if I'm not mistaken you're a bomb waiting to explode." He extended his hands and his palms were faced me. "And I mean that in the nicest way possible." He dropped his arms.

I laughed. "I'm good."

"You know your uncle helping me ride in the races," Paco said, skipping the subject, I think on purpose. "I beat twice last month because of him. Won twenty grand."

I nodded. "Good for you."

Paco cleared his throat.

"So you looking for work now?" Jace asked. "Because I could always use a man of your expertise in my crew." He looked toward the window. "And since I only see two cars out front, my Mercedes and a run down Honda, you could use the come up."

"He's out of the game," Kristen said. "Ain't you heard?"

"Whoa, you letting your lady talk for you these days?"

"Why I got to say anything when she does it best?" I looked him in the eyes. "You keep doing your thing and I'ma work at this father gig." I lifted one of Jace's ropes off his chest and let it fall down. "You always knew how to shine."

We walked out.

JACE

Jace watched Kalive limp to the car and open the door for Kristen. He redirected his attention to his cousin and Paco. "Did that nigga just try to play me?" Jace asked.

"You know he ain't that smart," Tony Wop said. "He's all muscle no brain."

"You know I don't ask for much right?" Jace continued.

"Sure don't," Paco, who was always on his dick, responded.

"Well both of you know we need a goon. Somebody who can do the dirty work so we don't have to get blood on our hands." He looked out the window again at the Honda, which was backing up. "Whoever can bring him to me in the best way possible will be handsomely compensated."

Tony Wop nodded. "I don't know about Pac' but I got an idea on how to handle the situation. So consider it done."

CHAPTER TWENTY-FIVE

KALI

Vaughn was helping me paint the nursery for my baby which I told Kristen was a boy. We didn't know the sex but I called it into existence.

I'm good for a son.

I can feel it.

All we had left was the ceiling but he was getting tired and started telling me how he understood why painters got big bucks. Since I didn't have no money to give him and told him in advance, I knew it was time for him to bounce.

"You can leave now, I'ma get up with you later." I put the roller in the bin filled with yellow paint. "I got the ceiling myself."

He squinted. "Hold up, you mad?"

"I feel like you hitting me up for bread when you know the situation."

"Wasn't nobody asking for money." He placed his roller in the bin. "Can't believe you in here getting mad over light shit. All I was saying was painting is hard work."

"Listen, you offered to help. Talking about you never had a relationship with Grams and wanted to do something to help me in her house."

"Man, can't nobody even say nothing around here." He walked over the plastic on the floor and flopped down on the green metal chair. "If you that hard up about money maybe you should do something to change it...like get at them streets."

"You know Kristen don't like that kind of talk in the house." I sat on the other chair. It wasn't until that moment that I realized I was tired too.

He ran his hands down his green fatigue pants. Yellow paint chips were all over his nails. "So I heard Jace stepped to you today."

I leaned back and crossed my arms over my chest. "How you hear about that?"

"Man, everybody around here know Jace want you on his squad. You been doing his dirty work for free since ya'll were kids."

"That was years ago and we ain't kids no more." I looked him dead in the eyes, wanting him to know I was serious. "The only thing on my mind is taking care of my girl and my baby. Jace can keep that gang banging shit over there."

"That's good, because at first I thought you were gonna always be on the nigga's dick."

Silence.

Vaughn moved uneasily. Must've felt I was a few seconds from stealing him in the jaw. "Didn't mean it that way, cousin. Just giving my opinion that's all."

"That's what I mean when I say you don't know what to say out your mouth."

He nodded. "You right...you right."

"Don't get me wrong, I fuck with Jace," I said. "When we were coming up he did a lot for me. And if I found out a nigga was genuinely trying to hurt him I would put him to rest. It's just that sometimes I feel like he's all about proving loyalty instead of what it really means."

"What you saying?"

"He questions who's with him too much. Anybody that gotta keep questioning if you fuck with them, after you've already put things on the line, don't know shit about real loyalty." I paused. "I have whipped niggas for him, stabbed niggas for him and all kind of other shit. Still he questions my love. He don't trust me and because of it I don't trust him. We never gonna be the same until he gives me a reason."

"So what you gonna do about paper? Babies need money, cousin."

"I gotta do me." I shrugged. "And we always alright."

"Ya'll hungry?" Kristen asked walking into the room. She looked around and smiled. "Oh my, God!" She rubbed her belly. "It's so pretty in here."

I stood up. "You can't be in here around these fumes." I softly pushed her out. "I told you that."

"You always so overprotective."

"And that ain't ever gonna change."

When there was a knock at the front door Kristen went to answer it and me and Vaughn followed. When I saw Sasha, whose prostitute name was Cherry walk inside, I shook my head. Kristen's cousin had a lot of shit with her and I told Kristen to be careful. But they were blood related so she got mad, causing me to stay out of it.

Sasha was pretty to look at but she never knew what to say out her mouth. Dark skin, short and petite, I could tell why dudes paid money to fuck her. The bitch was sexy.

"Hey, cousin." She hugged Kristen and Vaughn.

She tried to hug me and I said, "I'm good."

She laughed and shook her head. "Fuck it then." She looked at Vaughn. "I know you not about to leave when I just got here."

Vaughn grabbed his keys off the kitchen counter. "Yeah, got some things to take care of on the other side of town. I'ma get up with you later." He kissed her on the cheek and left.

"So what ya'll been doing in here? I haven't seen either of you in two months."

Kristen went into the kitchen and stirred the mashed potatoes cooking on the stove. I saw a meatloaf on the top and my stomach growled. "You know how Kali is. He don't want me doing nothing to jeopardize my health or this baby. Especially with me being due in any day now. So I've been staying low."

Kristen didn't catch Sasha roll her eyes but I did. I knew she was jealous of our relationship and I didn't like that shit. "Well let me see how far ya'll got in the nursery."

"I'm cooking," Kristen pouted. "Plus Kali doesn't want me back there."

"Then I guess he gonna have to show me." She grabbed me by the hand and pulled me in the back.

Kristen was smart, but I never understood why she didn't know her cousin was foul.

When we got into the room she closed the door and pushed me against the dry painted wall. Dropping to her knees she said, "Let me taste it," she moaned. "Please."

I pushed her back and her hand fell into the paint. "Bitch, don't ever in your life come at me like that, especially in my baby's room," I whispered. "You ain't taste my dick before so you ain't gonna do it now. Go choke, bitch."

She stood up, grabbed a towel off of the chair and wiped her hand. "You know what's so sad?"

"How 'bout you tell me, whore."

She laughed. "You a freak just like me." She stepped closer, leaned in and sniffed my shirt. "I smell it on you. If only you gave me a little bit you would see the fun we could have together. The magic we could make."

I walked away, to the other side of the room. "You don't know what you talking about."

"I'm perfect for you, Kali. My last name is Miller and everything. That means when we finally get married the only thing you gotta do is get your dick wet." She stuffed her hands in her jeans, pulled it back out and licked her finger.

My manhood jumped.

This bitch is trouble.

"What I want with a whore?"

"All that means for you is that my skills are perfected. I can do some things to you they haven't written about."

"What you doing here, Sasha? Stop the games."

She rolled her eyes. "Harmony been asking why you haven't been by her house." She paused. "You know she beefing with Jace and been sad. She wants all her friends around her."

"She need to be checking for the nigga Jace. I'm not her man."

"Don't fake, Kali. Everybody know you been secretly checking on that girl for years. You want her Spanish looking ass just like the rest of them niggas don't you?"

There she goes with the jealous shit when she doesn't have the right.

"I got who I want."

"We will see." She winked. "And if I know myself, it'll be sooner than later. I just hope you ready for Sasha's pussy because once you have this cherry you mine for life."

We were in our bed and Kristen was lying on her side, her back in my direction. My dick was inside of her tight pussy as I moved back and forth slowly. I know it was fucked up but when I closed my eyes I thought about Sasha's nasty ass. It was better than the thoughts of my mother that use to pop in my mind that I used every now and again to get off.

As I continued to fuck my girl I noticed her pussy was juicier and felt myself about to cum. "I love you, Kali," she moaned. "I'm glad you never gave up on me."

"I could never do that, I love you."

She moaned louder and hearing her soft voice made me feel guilty. I never fucked Sasha a day in my life but she stayed on my mind. I wanted my attention to remain on my bitch, where it should have been but every time I tried Sasha's face kept popping up.

I was taken back to a day when Sasha was sitting on my living room sofa. We were supposed to be watching a movie but the only thing she was watching was me. She was wearing a black mini skirt that sat on her upper thighs. Every time Kristen would get up, she would open her legs so I could see her pussy. On this day she was on her period so a white tampon string hung from between her pussy lips.

She must've known I liked it because she reached under her skirt, pulled it out and showed it to me. It dangled from left to right and the tip was tinged with just a little blood. I faked like I was mad but when I got up to use the bathroom I beat my dick until I came into the sink.

I had no intentions on fucking Sasha, but I would be lying if I said she didn't turn me on.

When my dick throbbed and I felt myself about to cum, I gripped Kristen's waist a little harder and exploded inside of her.

CHAPTER TWENTY-SIX
SASHA

*T*he mall was crowded as Kristen and Sasha walked through it toward another store. Sasha had so many bags you couldn't see the bottom of her legs. Kristen on the other hand had one plastic bag with strawberry socks inside.

"I said you can get it, Kristen," Sasha said with an attitude. "Just because you mommy-like don't mean you can't take gifts from family."

She looked at her. "What does that suppose to mean?"

They walked into Nordstrom's as Sasha rifled through her purse. "It means that fucking with a broke nigga got your mind twisted. You think this is how life's supposed to be. Now you don't even want to accept a pair of glasses from your cousin? I mean really...he did an outstanding job of reducing your standards."

"They were Versace, Sasha. I bring those glasses home and Kali gonna think that's what I want from him. And since he can't provide a lifestyle like that for me he's gonna go out and knock a few niggas over to make it happen. Maybe even you." She paused. "Is that what you really want?" She shook her head. "I knew I shouldn't have came to the mall. He didn't want me going anywhere this late in my pregnancy anyway."

"Oh, but you can pick his trifling ass up from the police station for stabbing his own leg?"

"All you need to know is I love mine, and mine loves me back."

Sasha's mood was consumed with jealousy...squinted eyes, a twitching jaw and a tense body. She could only dream of a love as strong as Kali and Kristen's. "What do you love about him anyway? Everybody says he likes the taste of blood."

She shrugged. "He does. And I love that about him too."

"Well whatever. Still don't make no sense to me."

Kristen grew angrier and snapped. "Bitch, it ain't got to make sense to you. Kali's my man. The last thing you should be trying to do is understand him."

"Wait...why you getting serious?"

"You coming at me about something that has nothing to do with you. My relationship is just that, mine." She pointed to herself.

"You know what, fuck it." She threw her hand in the air. "It's your life...if you want to waste it on a no good nigga I'll roll out the red carpet for you."

They continued to walk through Nordstrom's and were on their way out when Sasha stopped suddenly. "Hold up...I think I left my wallet in the shoe store." She patted her jean pockets and looked through her MCM purse again. "Go to the car, I'll be out in a sec." She handed Kristen her keys.

"Hurry up, I want to be home before Kali knows I'm missing."

"Bitch, wait, I'm coming," Sasha yelled.

Kristen shook her head and walked out of the mall, heading toward Sasha's silver Audi. Once she approached it she pressed the button to deactivate the alarm and tugged on the passenger door. When it wouldn't open she tugged it again and still it wouldn't budge. "Fuck is wrong with this car?"

Kristen was still struggling when she was struck over the back of the head. She fell face first into the ground and when she turned around she was staring into the eyes of the one man on the planet she never wanted to see again.

Her eyes widened when he aimed the barrel of a .45 at her belly. "Chris, please don't do this! Don't take my baby from me...I'm begging you!"

"You think I give a fuck about a baby you had with another nigga? You think I give a fuck about you? You left me for a bitch! You know what...I'm done talking to you."

Chris fired into her stomach before shooting at the center of her forehead.

"Why the fuck you get that nigga to do the job?" Jace yelled at Sasha as they sat in a dark alley inside of his Benz. "You don't hire somebody to do a murder with ties to the victim."

"Nobody's gonna guess he did it," Sasha said waving her hand. "Only a few people knew he was still tripping off of her 6 years later. I was one of them and the other was his mama. Trust me, he was the best person to do it. Be happy...it's done. Now you got Kali." She leaned back in her seat.

"I don't like it." He shook his head from side to side. "I don't like it at all."

She exhaled and her lips vibrated like she was a baby. "I'm sorry, I'm not understanding the problem. Tony said you wanted her taken care of and he talked to me. We good, relax."

"She was pregnant," he yelled. "When I said I wanted her gone I wasn't talking about dead!"

Sasha looked at him and laughed. "You may have them niggas who be jocking you fooled but I know the real Jace. You act all sweet but when it comes to blood you like it just like the rest of them niggas you roll with. The only thing you doing now is trying to avoid guilt."

"Something you don't have." He said in a low voice.

"What you talking about now?"

"She was your cousin, but you ain't have no problem putting a hit to take her out with her unborn baby."

She rolled her eyes and sat back in her seat. "It's done now, but it don't mean I didn't love my cousin."

Jace shook his head and ran his fingers through his curly hair. "Where this nigga at anyway? We can't let Kali find out about him from the streets. If he captures this nigga and tortures him it won't take Chris long to tell him about you and me."

"Apparently he already left town but I can find him for you. Of course if I do it's gonna cost you more money." She extended her hand and wiggled her fingers.

Jace dug into his pocket and held out a knot. When she tried to grab it he gripped her throat instead. "If I ever find out you said anything to Kali about this shit I will stick a thousand needles in your body and watch you die slowly, bitch." He let her go and smashed the money in her face.

She coughed a few times, tucked the money in her bra and looked at him. She wasn't as loose with the mouth as she was earlier. Rubbing her throat she said, "You've known your cousin all of your life. Tony wouldn't have come to me if he thought I couldn't hold water. I know shit about him you wouldn't believe, no matter what happens to me."

"You heard what I said, trick." He pointed in her face. "Get me the address, tell me where I can find this nigga. I'll do the rest."

It was two weeks after Kristen's funeral and Kali still hadn't been out of the house. Now he knew what his grandmother experienced when she lost his grandfather to death.

Standing in front of the full-length mirror in his grandmother's room, he examined the raised dog bite scars on his chest. They protruded and because no one took him to a doctor they healed like hard rocks. His body was a testament for the trials and tribulations he experienced in life.

By T. Styles

Born to irresponsible parents, they left him to be raised by two elderly people whose age would not allow the rearing he needed to be loved.

To have a solid foundation.

With Kristen gone there was nothing else alive that he cared for. He was a walking ball of hate waiting to expose itself to anyone in his path.

When his phone rang he answered. It was the first time since the funeral. "Hello."

"I know you want to be alone but I'm getting you out of the house and I will not take no for an answer."

Kali exhaled. "I'm not feeling a whole lot right now, Sasha. Kinda want to just chill in the – "

"Maybe I didn't make myself clear," she said aggressively. "I'm outside of your house waiting on you." He walked over to the window and she waved from her Audi. "So put a shirt on, nigga and come out because if you don't I'm coming in and you know I don't mind." She winked.

He hung up and shook his head. If nothing else she was persistent and it was probably the only way he would leave. Several nights he had visions of his grandparents calling him home. Telling him to come where they were because the road ahead was going to be difficult. They also told him that *unless he came with them, and took his own life that many, many men would die.*

He even felt a sense of peace in the notion that it was time for him to say goodbye to the world.

And then came Sasha.

He placed a white t-shirt on and walked over to the bed where his hatchet lay. It represented more than it's ability to take life. It belonged to the man who he considered his real father, whose life was snuffed out by its very blade. And then there was the strap, given to him by his grandfather.

Wearing the weapon wasn't about the fear it seemed to strike in those who saw him with it. It was more about the sentimentality and because of it he would carry it always.

Sasha's tight jean shorts were so small they could be panties. As she switched inside of her apartment, tossing the keys on the table, she worked extra hard to be sure he knew what she wanted.

To fuck.

"Lock the door," She told him. "I'ma grab some beers and go to the bathroom. Gotta shit, been holding it all day."

He tossed the green army bag his grandfather gave him on the floor that was filled with clean clothes and bolted the door. Still wondering what he was doing there he flopped on the sofa and observed her relaxed personality. She didn't seem like someone who lost their cousin just two and a half weeks earlier. Her lackadaisical attitude angered him and his jaw twitched. "Did you know she would be killed when she was with you?"

The beer accidently fell on the kitchen floor. Dropping to her knees, ass in his direction, he could see her pussy lips gripping the seat of the shorts. The opened canned beer made a fizz sound and she put it in the sink before grabbing two more. "Don't disrespect me like that, Kali. She was your girl but she was my blood relative."

"Well why you seem so cool with this shit?"

She walked into the living room and handed him one. "Everybody grieves differently."

He laughed. "You never really liked her. It was always about me when it came to you." He sat the beer on the floor.

Truthfully he didn't want it.

"I love my cousin but I would be lying if I said I didn't want her nigga." She placed her beer next to his on the floor and straddled him. He could feel the warmth from her pussy through his jeans. *Although he didn't fuck her physically, in his mind he touched her a million times.*

He ran his hand along the length of her neck and squeezed. Her eyes widened but it wasn't with fear, it was more like excitement. Although the two were not in love their strange fetishes made them compatible.

Sasha, like Kristen, loved men with violent tendencies. The only difference is when Kristen got pregnant she wanted him to change, to be more like a father while Sasha remained the same.

Kali on the other hand enjoyed inflicting pain on others, something he never did to Kristen outside of a few ass smacks pre-pregnancy period. She wasn't aware of his fetish because he did his best to hide his secrets so that her thoughts of him would remain pure.

"I will never love you, Sasha, no matter how much time we spend together." He squeezed harder. "Do you understand?"

She nodded and licked her lips. "Fuck me, Kali. Hurt me…please. I deserve it, I need it."

He stood up with her neck still in his hand. Her toes barely touched the cream carpet until he released, allowing her to fall to her knees. He bent down and slapped her so hard in the face her bottom lip bled.

By T. Styles

"This what you wanted right, bitch?" He slapped her again. "This what you been begging for right?"

She licked the blood away and said, "Harder...please."

Again he hit her until her face was so red his dick was throbbing. The more he acted out violently, the more she begged. He realized Sasha was right all along. Although they weren't suited in a relationship, behind closed doors they were in sync.

When she was sore and bruised, he ripped her shorts off exposing her purple thongs. Forcing her on all fours he unbuckled his pants and pushed into her asshole. He could feel a blockage and remembered she said she had to shit earlier.

"Kali, don't do it there, I have to go to the bathroom."

"Shut up, bitch. I'ma fuck you like I want and you gonna take it too." He gripped the back of her hair. "You understand?"

She nodded. "Yes, sir."

When he removed his dick he noticed it was covered lightly with brown stool and grabbed her by the hair. "Now suck it off."

Although the feces came from her own body, and she was as freaky as they came, this was too much for even her.

But the look in his eyes told her the last thing she could do was refuse.

She wanted the man and now she had him.

In all of his insanity.

She obeyed and tried her best not to throw up as her tongue ran up and down his shaft. He was so turned on that he was minutes away from busting. When she was done he put her on fours again and licked her asshole clean, tasting the remnants of her feces in the process.

He had never done anything like that before but he was sure he would do it again. The nastiness of the sex and the way Sasha took dick on command had him seconds from exploding.

It was the best sex in his life.

He reinserted his soiled stiffness into her pussy and sexed her from the back. "Fuckkkkkk," he yelled. "This thing is just right."

Sasha breathed heavily, her pussy-dripping wet. She had come along time ago when he ate her ass so she was good. "You like that, Kali? Take it, baby. You belong there."

"Fuck," he moaned one last time before exploding inside of her.

When he was done he stood up and buckled his pants. "Now tell me what I'm really doing here. And don't play games."

Kali sat in the passenger seat of Jace's car, with Tony Wop, Kreshon and Paco in the back. They scooped him earlier from Sasha's under the disguise of getting him to have a good time since he lost his girl. At first he was skeptical but Jace talked a fair game. Reminded him that with Kristen and his grandparents gone, essentially he was all the family Kali had left.

Jace laid the groundwork but now it was time to get down to business.

"I know this ain't the right time, man, but I need your help," Jace said. He pulled over in front of an abandoned house.

Kalive was uncomfortable with Jace's sudden mood shift but rested easy because if any of them tried to fuck him over, at least one of them would kiss the blade, which sat in his lap. "What's up?"

"First I want to tell you that I always considered us to be family. We practically grew up together and I love you. Shit, my girl even fucks with you." He laughed. "Harmony be worried more about this nigga than me sometimes."

Paco and Tony Wop broke out in hard laughter but quieted when it was obvious that Jace wasn't as amused.

"I thought we were off the family topic." Kali wasn't feeling the fluffing up act Jace was doing anymore. He always knew Jace as a straight shooter and preferred him to keep it that way. "What do you need? Just ask." His question was slow and controlled.

Jace nodded. "I see you want to get right down to business so allow me. As you already know my pops trusting me with the operation out here. With him living in LA he don't have time to worry about the shops in DC, but it doesn't mean he's not up on what's going on. And I don't want to let him down."

"The other day some niggas knocked down the door of this house," Paco said pointing at the run down tenement. "They took everything we had...money, drugs and respect."

"After they hit us of course they got ghost," Jace added. "And we didn't have eyes on them until now. Tomorrow we already got a plan in the works to snatch up Bam, but getting at Star, his partner, is another problem."

"Who stole the money?" Kali asked.

"Bam and his people," Jace said. "But we want Star too."

"You don't know where he is?" Kali asked, readjusting in the comfortable luxury car.

"We know where the nigga is, but they would see my immediate crew coming. We need somebody who can slide in undetected. Someone he doesn't know and that someone is you."

"So you think if we got Star, Bam will tell you where your stash and money are?" Kali asked.

"Yes," Jace replied.

"I never heard of a nigga given up the stolen goods for a partner," Kali said. "Doesn't Bam have someone closer to him? Someone he loves?"

"His kid goes to Nalle Elementary but we think if we get Star, between the two of them somebody will say something. Ain't no need in bringing kids in the picture at this point."

"How old is the girl?" Kali asked.

"About seven or eight," Tony shrugged. "Who gives a fuck? The focus here is Star."

Kali already didn't like Tony and hated when he interjected but he bit his tongue. Without a girl or a baby to love he was a free agent and it was time to get his blade wet.

They continued to give him the details on where to find Star but Kali tapped out a long time ago. The only thing on his mind was Kristen and the baby she carried in her belly before their lives were snuffed out. He imagined how it would have been to hold his child. To watch it grow to it's highest potential.

Now he had nothing.

If he couldn't have his kid, he didn't give a fuck about anybody else's. In his opinion if Bam wanted in the game having his kid snatched up came with the territory.

"The best part about it is with you being 17 even if they catch you, they gotta charge you as a juvenile," Jace said.

Kali was 19 but he let him run his mouth since he thought he knew everything. Besides, he had no intentions on getting caught.

"You got all that?" Jace asked. "Because it looks like you out of it."

Kali already knew what he was going to do so he nodded. In his mind both plans would lead to the return of the stash so who cared? "I got it."

"Good, because I told you we were family but it's time that I do something for you. Something that proves my loyalty because you have always put yourself out there for me." He paused. "And that something is in the house waiting."

Kali sat up and looked over at him. "What is it?"

"The nigga who killed Kristen," Tony said. "The fellas roughed him up a little bit but other than that he's whole."

"Yeah, the only thing missing is his tongue," Jace said.

Kali couldn't believe he was standing over Chris' weakened body. He was strapped to a chair that had the legs bolted into the ground so it wouldn't move. It was clearly made for torture, which Kali planned to take full advantage.

Jace, Paco and Kreshon were behind him, to ensure Chris didn't say anything with his stub of a tongue that was audible enough to finger them for being responsible for the hit on her life.

Years ago, after Kali fought Chris straight up and won, Grand warned him about leaving him alive. And to find out that he was responsible for his girlfriend's death consumed him with more rage. If only he had listened his precious wifey would be alive.

Kalive could've walked down the steps, shot him in the head and went on with life but he wanted to make the moment last.

The fact that Jace went so far to find out who killed Kristen made Kali indebted and he would do all he could in the future to prove his love to his oldest friend.

Jace was now closer to Kali than a brother.

First Kali sliced X's up and down his thighs and on the tops of his feet. Chris' inaudible pleas were starting to become annoying so Kali kicked off his own Nike removed his white sock and stuffed it in Chris's throat. With the place a little quieter, he chopped off each of his toes before moving to his fingers.

Jace who didn't have the stomach for persecution rushed back up the stairs, claiming he needed air. Paco and Kreshon chose to watch the levels of depravity Kali would ascend to.

When his toes and fingers were gone he sliced off his ears, followed by the soft tissue of his nose. Kalive took pleasure in the pain he was causing and moreover, in the satisfaction he was experiencing at getting revenge.

When he was tired, and two hours had gone by leaving Chris hanging onto life, he removed his hatchet and raised it high in the air, bringing it crashing down into the center of his skull.

With the work done Kali dropped to his knees and wept. The pain of losing all those he cared about rushed over him. "I'm so sorry, Kristen. I'm so fucking sorry!"

His pain went on for a minute before suddenly stopping. He rose to his feet, dusted off his knees and looked at Paco and Kreshon. Words were not needed but they got the message. If either of them told a soul about his moment of weakness, they would suffer too.

One only needed to look at Chris' corpse to know that Kali was anything but playing.

He couldn't believe his luck when he walked into the hallway of Nalle Elementary and saw Bam's daughter alone. Class was in session so the hall was empty. She was humming to *herself and he noticed the baby blue dress she wore was stained with orange juice.*

On the hunt, the moment she walked inside the bathroom he followed her. Patiently he waited for her to finish peeing and when she came out he grabbed her from behind and slapped his hand over her mouth just before she screamed. His face was concealed in a ski mask, which made the horror worse for the child.

"Shut up," he whispered harshly, his hand pressing on her mouth harder. "Do you hear me? Shut up!"

She squirmed uncontrollably and he was thinking of knocking her out with a blow to the face but the door opened and a first grade teacher, Mrs. Hammond, walked inside. "Dear God," she said covering her mouth when she saw the masked man.

Instead of running she stepped closer and Kali aimed the .45, which sat in a holster on his hip, in her direction. For a job like this his hatchet wouldn't be as effective so he opted for the hammer instead. "Don't move, bitch!" he warned. "Unless you want to be splattered."

The woman's body trembled although courage was in her eyes. She remained still. "Sir, I don't know you. And I don't know what's going on or why you feel the need to take that child. Maybe her father is responsible, since I hear he's a drug dealer."

"Shut the fuck up!" Kali yelled.

She trembled and cried harder. "I don't mean to upset you. All I'm asking is that you please not take her away from her mother. There is no worse feeling then having a child kidnapped."

"What about one that's murdered? In a parking lot? While still in the mother's womb?"

She nodded as tears continued to roll down her face. "You're right, son. And judging by the sound of your voice I can tell you're young. You'll have many more kids. And I know you gonna do what you want anyway. But I must tell you that if you take this little girl, if you kidnap her from this school, the karma you will suffer will stay with you for all the days of your life. You will never find peace. Not in life and not with your children. Is that what you want?"

"Karma already came to me," he said coldly. He approached the woman, the child still in hand. Common sense told him to kill her because he was certain by the time she left the bathroom the area would be swarming with cops. But he gave her credit for being brave, far braver than his mother ever was.

So with the little girl in one hand, he brought down the butt of the gun on the top of her head, knocking her out. When she dropped to the floor he walked over her body and ran out.

Two minutes later he tossed the child in the trunk of the car, her mouth and hands duct taped. Quickly he eased into the passenger seat where his cousin Vaughn was waiting with the car running. "You alright, cousin?" Vaughn asked.

The guilt of what he'd done was heavy. "Yeah, take me to Jace's crib."

By T. Styles

CHAPTER TWENTY-SEVEN

PRESENT DAY

Three men waited for the cargo to step off the van...

One tall and white, the other fat and Mexican and the last black and short. No matter their sizes they all held high-powered assault weapons in case the men wanted drama.

"Remember what I said," Kali whispered to Barrie once more as they exited the van. "Trip me so I can get the gun under the—"

"He's got a gun!" Timo yelled, alerting the abductors. "It's under the van and they planning to use it on you!"

"Timo, you a fucking snake!" Barrie yelled. "If I didn't have my hands tied I would fuck you up. I can't believe this shit!"

Kali thought it was awful funny that now that Timo was scared, the stuttering ceased.

"And his hands are untied too!" Timo continued his snitching rant.

A tall white man with missing teeth yanked the men from the van and snatched the do rags off of each of their eyes. The bright light from the moon felt blinding as the mosquitoes fought desperately for territory on their heated torsos.

Tall White turned Kali around and reviewed his binds, which were unraveled. He readjusted them so tightly Kali's palms turned white. "Where is the fucking gun?" he asked through clenched teeth.

"I don't know what you talking about!" Kali lied.

"Give me the fuckin gun!" Tall White yelled, spit flying in Kali's face.

"It's under the van," Timo continued, carrying on like the snitch he was obviously born to be.

Tall White handed his assault rifle to Short Black, dropped to his knees and looked under the van. He was down for a minute before emerging with a .9-millimeter handgun, which he brought down over Kali's head, causing blood to ooze into a stream down the center of his face.

Barrie and Kali were disgusted with Timo's betrayal.

Timo moved excitedly. "You see, I told you what he was doing! Can you let me go now?" Timo begged. "I don't deserve to be out here with them. I want to be with my family." His eyes were wide and it looked like he was on drugs. "I don't even know what I did wrong!"

"So stupid," Kali said. "I told you these niggas don't negotiate!"

Tall White walked up to Timo and smiled. He placed a heavy hand on his shoulder and squeezed. "Great job. We could've been hurt if things worked out to Kali's favor and for that you should be rewarded."

Timo looked at Barrie and grinned. "Look who's stupid now?"

Barrie shook his head and the sympathy he felt for his naive brother-in-law was written over his face. Neither Kali nor Barrie thought it would end well for him.

Tall White was handed his gun and he pressed the barrel against Timo's forehead. "This may not seem like a reward but if you knew what we had planned you would agree that it is."

"No, please don't!" Timo screamed before the trigger was tugged, his brain exploded and he flopped to the ground. Gunpowder wafted in the air and blood splatters slapped against Kali and Barrie's faces.

Tall White turned to his men and The Mexican Man cut on a large yellow flashlight that illuminated the path before them, while Short Black dragged Timo's corpse.

"Get to walking!" Tall White yelled.

Barrie and Kali walked through the woods, side by side. Rocks and branches cut into their feet as they stepped further into the forest. Tall White and his men continued behind them, but not so close that they could make out their conversation. There was no need to be very close because their bullets could reach them no matter where they ran.

The strange sound of crickets chirping made the experience seem darker.

"I do have something I regret," Kali said to Barrie.

"What you talking about?"

"In the van, we were talking about regrets and I do have one."

"Now you tell me," Barrie responded under his breath.

"You want to hear it or not?" Blood rolled down the middle of Kali's eyes and sat at the top of his lips. He licked it off.

Barrie thought the man looked insane but what else was he going to do? In a minute he would be dead. "Not sure if confessing to me will make things better but go ahead."

"I kidnapped a little girl once when I was a teenager. Her father owed a partner of mine a debt. I wasn't even supposed to have her but my life was so fucked up I didn't care about a child."

Barrie looked at him with raised brows. "You killed her?"

Kali nodded.

"How old was she?"

"About seven."

Barrie shrugged. "If her father was in the game and he owed money that's part of the hustle. Can't blame the killers without blaming the players."

"But that wasn't the reason I did it." Kali took a deep breath. "I did it because a nigga murdered my girl and my unborn child. They found her body in the parking lot of a mall, like she was trash. So I took my anger out on a lot of people and the kid was one of my casualties." He exhaled. "I heard once that hell comes to pedophiles and children killers. If so I'm doomed."

Barrie's eyes widened and he seemed afraid.

"Stop right there!" Tall White yelled when they approached a huge pile of dirt on the other side of a large unmarked grave. Short Black tossed Timo's body inside.

"You see the hole, now crawl in it!" he said to Kali and Barrie.

Kali turned toward Tall White. "Before you kill me can you at least tell me what I did?" he pleaded. "A man has a right to know why he's being sentenced to death."

Tall White laughed. "Get in the fucking hole."

Kali stepped into the grave, which was deeper than he thought. As he dropped inside he almost broke his ankle underestimating the depth. It was also wide enough for three men to lie shoulder to shoulder. While they lay side-by-side, Timo's corpse at their feet, Short Black picked up a shovel and began throwing dirt over their bodies.

"Wait, you not even gonna shoot us first?" Barrie yelled, his voice squeaky. He had come to terms with dying but suffocating was not in his mind. "You gonna bury us alive?"

Tall White and The Mexican smiled as Short Black continued to throw dirt over them.

"I can't believe I'm gonna die like this," he said starting to lose control. "I can't...I can't..." he was hyperventilating and losing himself.

"Nothing we can do about it now but pray, man," Kali said. "It's over."

Barrie started crying as the dirt continued to slap them in the faces. "I did something too," Barrie said looking over at Kali. "I mean I did a lot of shit but one thing fucks me up 'cause I don't understand why."

"What you talking about?" Kali asked, turning his face to the side so the dirt wouldn't hit him in the eyes.

"I...I buried a bitch and her kid in a shed behind my house. Underground." He cried. "You said hell comes to children killers so I'm doomed too."

"If they in a shed, maybe somebody will find them," Kali reasoned.

"Not the way it's built. If you walk...if you walk in it looks like a regular floor but if you move a few things aside you'll see the door to the underground. They were in there for two days and they gonna die without food and water."

Kali frowned. "Why you do that?"

"The person who hired me wanted them to die slow. I've killed many men in my life but I hated this job. Nobody deserves that kind of death."

"Why take it?"

"I didn't know what he wanted until after I spent the money."

Kali exhaled and waved his hand. Suddenly the dirt stopped falling. Barrie thought he was losing his mind when Tall White helped Kali out of the grave and handed him his hatchet and strap. He slipped it on and then was given a cell phone. He dialed a number and gave whoever was on the other line the information Barrie had given him. When he was done he handed the phone back to Tall White.

"What the fuck is going on?" Barrie yelled, looking up to him.

"I'm not going to lie," Kali said calmly. "While I'm relieved to know where my family is, so that I can give them a proper burial, I'm disappointed in you."

"What…why?"

"My plan was to kill you slowly to find out where my kid was but time was not on my side. People told me that you've been tortured and even kidnapped in the past to reveal the places of the bodies you disposed of. Through it all you never told a soul. Until now." Kali pointed down at him. "But then somebody said something that stuck. They said the things you knew you would take to your grave, so I took you to it."

Barrie thought he was in the twilight zone. "I'm confused, so you, you know these men?"

When the cell phone Kali was just using rang, Tall White answered. He nodded and extended it to Kali. "Sir, it's for you."

He was just cracking him over the head. Now he's calling him sir? Barrie thought.

Barrie couldn't believe that he witnessed Kali being beaten and bruised just to find his family. He was afraid and respected him all at once because of the lengths he had gone through. He never met a more vicious killer.

"Yes," Kali said into the phone. He exhaled deeply. "Wait for me, I'm on the way." He handed the phone back to Tall White.

"What's going to happen to me?" Barrie asked.

"What do you think?"

He swallowed. "My wife…before they took me she was in bed sick. Is she…is she okay?"

Kali nodded yes.

"Thank you," He exhaled. "Thank you."

"Because I respect you, and I know this was not your doing, I'm going to give you two options. Tell me who paid you and I will give you a quick death. Refuse to tell me and I'll bury you alive." He paused. "Decide."

Barrie pissed on himself, dampening the dirt under his body.

Kali, along with Tall White, The Mexican, Short Black and three other men, successfully pushed a freezer filled with bricks off the door leading to the underground within Barrie's shed.

Once it was out of the way Kali pried the door open by slamming at the lock with the hatchet. Before long the door was open and he yanked it up and rushed down the steps.

It was dark and dank but The Mexican lit his flashlight as they moved deeper into the hole. It didn't take long to find Madjesty and Cassius's bodies in the corner of a dirt wall. She was holding her son and it was obvious that they both were dead.

Kali dropped to his knees and cried for the second time since Kristen was killed. He wept for the things he'd done in the past and all of the things he would do in the future. But most of all he wept because his daughter, who he had grown to love was murdered with her child.

His grandson.

While everyone else stayed behind Kali, afraid to move closer out of respect, Tall White bravely approached the bodies. He bent down and examined them. With a smile on his face he turned around and said, "Sir...I think they're alive."

"What?"

"They're alive! I think they're alive!"

Mad stirred a little in the hospital bed and when she peeled her eyes open Kali popped up from the chair he'd been nursing for three days. He placed her black baseball cap over her long curly hair and held her hand. "How you feel?"

She smiled. "Pops." Her tongue felt heavy, her mouth pasty. "What you doing here?"

Her strong breath hit him in the face and he waved the air. "Whoa," he said playfully. "The first thing I'm gonna get you is a toothbrush."

She laughed but stopped when her throat hurt. "What happened?" She looked around again. "What am I doing here?"

Kali grew serious. "You were kidnapped with my grand boy. But don't worry, I'm gonna handle everything. All you have to do is relax."

Her eyes grew wide and she popped up. A sharp pain radiated through her stomach causing her to lie back down. "Where is Cassius? Where is my son?"

"He's in the PICU unit."

Her eyes watered. "I remember now...we were...we were looking at a new house, me and my friends. When somebody came from behind us and put a black bag over my head. At first I thought it was just me they took until I heard Cassius crying too." Tears rolled down her face. "Pops, please say he's okay."

"He's alive, Kid. He's alive, and that's all we can stand on now." When he saw her losing control his brows lowered. "You and your boy were kidnapped, Kid. If things went the way the person wanted you'd be dead but you're not. Tears not gonna help us for what we have to do next. Are you gonna cry or fight? That's all I want to know."

Ann cruised down the highway with Kali in the passenger seat and Madjesty in the back. Every now and again he would turn around and look at Mad but her gaze remained outside, with the brim of her hat pressed against the window. She reminded him of himself when he was a kid. Young and looking for his parents to protect him.

The only thing is they never did.

"I've been thinking, Mad. I don't want you to come with me today."

She rolled her head from the window and looked up at him. "But I need to be there." She frowned. "I need to see him tell me that he did it and why."

"You know why. Jace left you and his daughter a million dollars, and he wanted half. There's not a whole lot more to it."

"I gotta go, Pops."

"I never told you how I grew up. Never wanted to say much about my past because thinking about it made me angry and violent." He exhaled. "But I'm talking about it now because I see what's ahead for you. I see your life is about to mirror mine so closely I won't be able to tell our paths apart."

Ann looked over at Kali and back at the road. Once Jace's girl, she'd been with Kali for many years and he never opened up to her. So hoping to get more insight on a man she adored she decreased her speed.

"I was abandoned by my mother and father. He spent most of his life in a mental institution. He's in one now."

"You in contact with your father?" Mad asked with raised brows. "Why you never told me?"

He shrugged. "It's nothing to tell. He has the title but he wasn't a man. I put money on the facility each month but I don't see him." He exhaled. "What I'm trying to say is that I was born into hate, Mad. I didn't have a choice, that's the life I was given. But it's not too late for you. You have a woman who loves you, a kid who's fighting in the hospital who needs you present. Don't come to hell with me. Go back while you still can."

She exhaled. "I know you're trying to protect me."

"I'm doing for you what I would have wanted my parents to do for me."

"And I'm protecting my son too, Pops. Them mothafuckas took Cassius and me, threw us underground and left us for dead. I can't let this shit slide."

"You're my kid, Madjesty. Let me handle this. I'm begging you."

She looked into his eyes and pressed her head against the window again. "What you don't get is this…I'm already in hell."

Rick sat at a beautiful pearl colored table for two with his granddaughter Jayden in the backyard of his mansion. The sun was not at it's highest and a cool breeze provided comfort for the two. "Granddaddy, I don't believe you," Jayden giggled. "You can't sneak food into the movie theater."

He picked up his wheat toast, took a bite and laughed with his mouth full. "You can do anything you want if you got money." He placed the food down. "You of all people should know that." He paused. "Besides, I hate movie theater food. If you and I are going on a date tonight then my granddaughter will have the best...steak!" he clapped his hands together.

Although his joke was dry Jayden was thoroughly amused. Suddenly her laughter simmered. "Granddad, I've been having bad dreams lately."

"About what, honey?"

"My girls." She moved uneasily in her seat. "I think they're getting money on the side."

By T. Styles

"Explain the business and I'll give any advice I can." He crossed his legs and attempted to pick food out of his teeth with his tongue.

"I get a call for a girl." She paused. "The client pays with a credit card in advance and the girl meets him, always with one of my escorts. If the client likes the girl and wants to see her again, they usually offer a tip which I give to my girl."

"Sounds organized enough, even though I wouldn't use a credit card for this line of business. The bigger the paper trail the more likely the government will come calling."

"It's an unmarked business. It doesn't have my name associated with it anywhere."

He tilted his head to the side but still wasn't a fan. "Go ahead."

"Well lately there's been less tips and some of my favorite clients have stopped calling. They claim to be focused on their marriages but I'm not buying it. These are the kind of men who love pussy and not having it messes with their marriages and businesses."

He nodded in agreement. "I've said it many times that nothing does a marriage better than an affair."

She smiled.

"Tell me...how many days do your whores have off?"

"Two?"

He laughed. "That's one day too many. Cut their time to one day a week and make sure another girl, someone you trust the most, is with them at all times. Even on their off days." He pointed at her. "Never let your whores get too far from your grasp. You'll lose them forever."

Jayden was smiling until she saw Kali and Madjesty walking up behind Rick like they were mad men. Kali was holding a pillowcase soaked with blood and Jayden looked as if she saw a ghost. "Granddaddy." She said shivering.

He followed her eyesight and almost relieved his bowels when he saw them approaching. "Johnson! Greggs!" He called out toward the house. "Johnson and Greggs!"

Kali walked closer and tossed the bloody bag on the table. "If you're calling your men who're supposed to be protecting you don't bother. Their hands are in the bag and the rest of them is in the foyer."

Madjesty looked into Jayden's eyes, never blinking once. It had been a long time since she'd seen her. Ever since Mad won custody of her own son in court, after receiving half of the million-dollar insurance policy Jace left in her name, Jayden had been bitter.

She wanted the little boy for herself and Rick wanted the money.

Their entire life was something for the movies.

First Jace and Kali slept with Harmony while she was ovulating resulting in both of their eggs implanting. Although twins who shared a mother, Jace was Jayden's father and Kali was Madjesty's. Since Madjesty was not Jace's biological daughter, when Jace died, Rick didn't understand why he would leave her half of a million dollar insurance policy.

With him losing everything he owned from gambling, and relying on his granddaughter's whore hustle to stay afloat, he wanted the money for himself. After attempting to bully Madjesty into signing it over failed he had her kidnapped with an order to not kill her quickly, instead let her and the kid die slowly.

That's where Barrie came in.

"Why?" Madjesty asked walking up to Rick. "Why would you have me and my son kidnapped?" She was so angry she was shaking. "You would do all of this shit just so you can get money Jace left me?" she screamed. "My son is in the hospital fighting for his life and it's all your fault!"

She hit him in the face and when he tried to strike back Kali brought the hatchet down on the table, shattering it completely.

Rick and Jayden jumped.

Rick rubbed his jaw. "I don't know what you're talking about."

"Granddaddy," Jayden said softly. "Is this true? Did you have them kidnapped?"

Rick stared at her and Kali tried desperately to read his expression.

"If you were kidnapped it had nothing to do with me," Rick said slamming his fist on the already fractured table. He was so busy expressing anger that he didn't see Kali follow up with the hatchet, the blade cutting into his wrist bone.

"Ouuchhhh!" Rick screamed and squirmed out of the chair, holding his bloody stump but Kali followed him because he wasn't done.

"First you ruined my father's life," Kali said. "Your product was the reason he and my mother couldn't take care of their responsibilities. You took them from me but you will not take my kid too."

Kali swung the hatchet again and the blade tore into Rick's throat. His eyes widened as he held the gaping wound with his good hand. Blood sprouted all over the patio.

And then he took his last breath.

Kali moved toward Jayden, getting ready to cut her down too when Madjesty stood in front of her. "No, Pops." She extended her hand and pushed him back slowly.

Kali's eyes widened. "Kid, she was involved." He pointed at Jayden with the hatchet, blood dripping off the blade. "You gonna leave her alive? And let her get away with it?"

Madjesty looked at Jayden, her twin sister. So much happened to cause their bond to fracture but she couldn't see her being responsible for almost killing her nephew. Jayden may have hated her but she didn't think she was capable of harming Cassius too. "Did you know that he kidnapped me and your nephew? And left us to die slowly underground?"

"I don't know what you're talking about," Jayden said softly, placing her hand over her heart. "But I need you to know that I would never do anything to hurt you or my nephew. Before you came back into the picture I raised him, Madjesty." She pointed at herself. "As my own." Tears rolled down her face. "I loved my grandfather, I still do now. But if he did anything to harm you or Cassius he deserved what you delivered and I will not stand in the way."

The more she talked, the more Kali didn't trust her.

"Is Cassius okay?" Jayden asked.

Madjesty looked at her and then at Kali. "Come on, Pops. Let's go."

He remained planted, his eyes on Jayden. "I think we should kill her, Mad. I don't trust her." His voice was firm.

"And I'm telling you that I can't do that." She exhaled. "But if you want to, knowing how I feel about it, then you can do whatever. I gotta go check on my son." Madjesty pulled her hat down further over her eyes and walked away.

Kali moved closer to Jayden, raised his hatchet and ran it alongside her face. Rick's blood on her chin.

Just a second ago she was grief stricken and now she was grinning like a Cheshire cat. "Do it, and watch her hate you forever," Jayden said.

"We gonna have our day again," Kali said calmly. "The kid may be green but I know a snake when I kill one."

Kali looked at her once more and walked away.

THE END

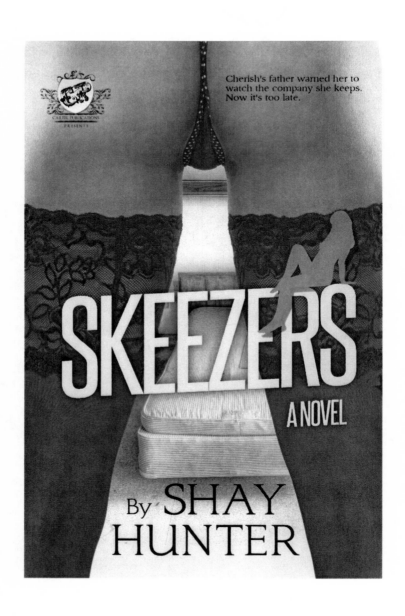

Cherish's father warned her to
watch the company she keeps.
Now it's too late.

SKEEZERS

A NOVEL

By SHAY HUNTER

The Cartel Publications Order Form
www.thecartelpublications.com
Inmates **ONLY** receive novels for $10.00 per book.
(Mail Order **MUST** come from inmate directly to receive discount)

Shyt List 1	_____	$15.00
Shyt List 2	_____	$15.00
Shyt List 3	_____	$15.00
Shyt List 4	_____	$15.00
Shyt List 5	_____	$15.00
Pitbulls In A Skirt	_____	$15.00
Pitbulls In A Skirt 2	_____	$15.00
Pitbulls In A Skirt 3	_____	$15.00
Pitbulls In A Skirt 4	_____	$15.00
Victoria's Secret	_____	$15.00
Poison 1	_____	$15.00
Poison 2	_____	$15.00
Hell Razor Honeys	_____	$15.00
Hell Razor Honeys 2	_____	$15.00
A Hustler's Son 2	_____	$15.00
Black and Ugly As Ever	_____	$15.00
Year Of The Crackmom	_____	$15.00
Deadheads	_____	$15.00
The Face That Launched A	_____	$15.00
Thousand Bullets		
The Unusual Suspects	_____	$15.00
Miss Wayne & The Queens of DC	_____	$15.00
Paid In Blood (eBook Only)	_____	$15.00
Raunchy	_____	$15.00
Raunchy 2	_____	$15.00
Raunchy 3	_____	$15.00
Mad Maxxx	_____	$15.00
Quita's Dayscare Center	_____	$15.00
Quita's Dayscare Center 2	_____	$15.00
Pretty Kings	_____	$15.00
Pretty Kings 2	_____	$15.00
Pretty Kings 3	_____	$15.00
Silence Of The Nine	_____	$15.00
Silence Of The Nine 2	_____	$15.00
Prison Throne	_____	$15.00
Drunk & Hot Girls	_____	$15.00
Hersband Material	_____	$15.00
The End: How To Write A	_____	$15.00
Bestselling Novel In 30 Days (Non-Fiction Guide)		
Upscale Kittens	_____	$15.00

KALI: Raunchy Relived

Wake & Bake Boys	_____	$15.00
Young & Dumb	_____	$15.00
Young & Dumb 2:	_____	$15.00
Tranny 911	_____	$15.00
Tranny 911: Dixie's Rise	_____	$15.00
First Comes Love, Then Comes Murder	_____	$15.00
Luxury Tax	_____	$15.00
The Lying King	_____	$15.00
Crazy Kind Of Love	_____	$15.00
And They Call Me God	_____	$15.00
The Ungrateful Bastards	_____	$15.00
Lipstick Dom	_____	$15.00
A School of Dolls	_____	$15.00
KALI: Raunchy Relived	_____	$15.00

Please add $4.00 **PER BOOK** for shipping and handling.

The Cartel Publications * P.O. BOX 486 OWINGS MILLS MD 21117

Name: _____

Address: _____

City/State: _____

Contact# & Email:

_____

Please allow 5-7 BUSINESS days before shipping.

The Cartel Publications is NOT responsible for prison orders rejected.

NO PERSONAL CHECKS ACCEPTED

STAMPS NO LONGER ACCEPTED

By T. Styles

CPSIA information can be obtained at www.ICGtesting.com
Printed in the USA
LVOW07s1835240116

471937LV00001BA/23/P

9 780996 209908